BIONICLE®

#4 Trial by Fire

GREG FARSHTEY
Writer
RANDY ELLIOTT
Artist

PAPERCUTZ™

NEW YORK

Trial by Fire

GREG FARSHTEY – Writer
RANDY ELLIOTT— Artist
TOBY DUTKIEWICZ – Art Director/Design
PETER PANTAZIS — Colorist
KEN LOPEZ, NICK J. NAPOLITANO – Letterers
JAYE GARDNER – Original Editor
JOHN McCARTHY – Production
MICHAEL PETRANEK – Editorial Assistant
JIM SALICRUP
Editor-in-Chief

ISBN 10: 1-59707-132-3 paperback edition
ISBN 13: 978-1-59707-132-1 paperback edition
ISBN 10: 1-59707-133-1 hardcover edition
ISBN 13: 978-1-59707-133-8 hardcover edition
LEGO, the LEGO logo and BIONICLE are trademarks of the LEGO Group.
Manufactured and distributed by Papercutz under license from the LEGO Group.
© 2003, 2009 The LEGO Group. All rights reserved.
Originally published as comicbooks by DC Comics as BIONICLE #22-27.
Editorial matter © 2009 Papercutz.
Printed in China.
Distributed by Macmillan.
10 9 8 7 6 5 4 3 2 1

TRIAL BY FIRE
CHAPTER ONE

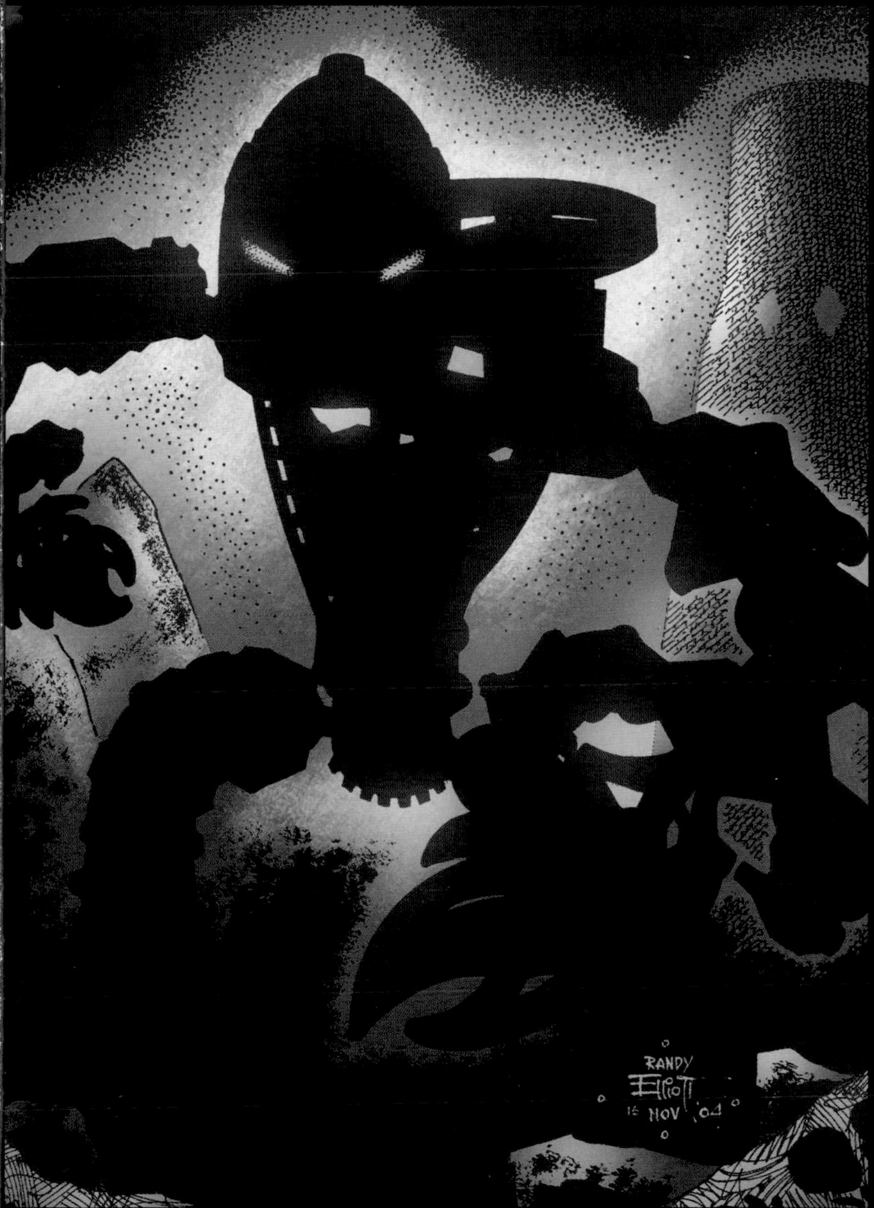
RANDY
ELLIOTT
15 NOV '04

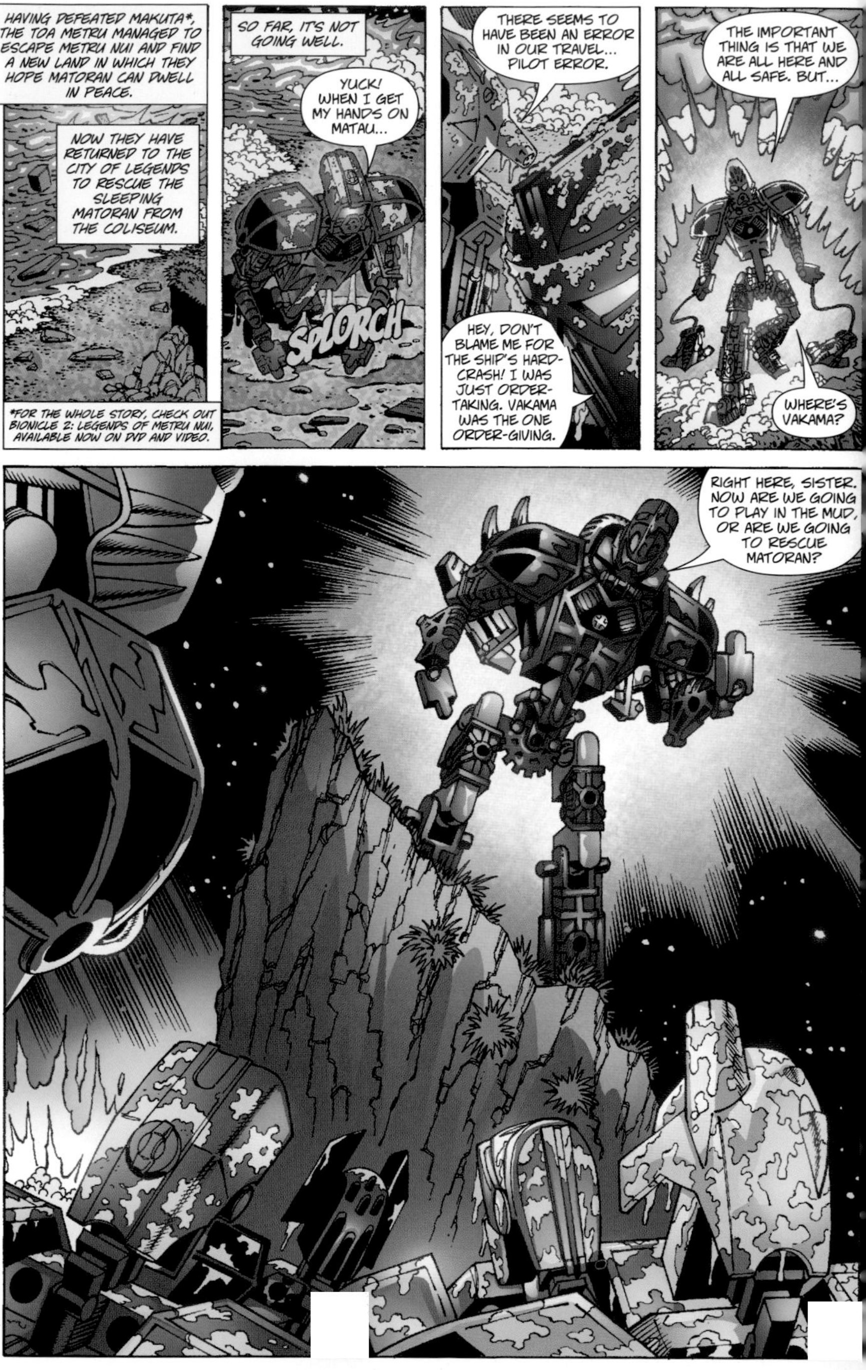

HAVING DEFEATED MAKUTA*, THE TOA METRU MANAGED TO ESCAPE METRU NUI AND FIND A NEW LAND IN WHICH THEY HOPE MATORAN CAN DWELL IN PEACE.
NOW THEY HAVE RETURNED TO THE CITY OF LEGENDS TO RESCUE THE SLEEPING MATORAN FROM THE COLISEUM.
*FOR THE WHOLE STORY, CHECK OUT BIONICLE 2: LEGENDS OF METRU NUI, AVAILABLE NOW ON DVD AND VIDEO.
SO FAR, IT'S NOT GOING WELL.
YUCK! WHEN I GET MY HANDS ON MATAU...
SPLORCH
THERE SEEMS TO HAVE BEEN AN ERROR IN OUR TRAVEL... PILOT ERROR.
HEY, DON'T BLAME ME FOR THE SHIP'S HARD-CRASH! I WAS JUST ORDER-TAKING. VAKAMA WAS THE ONE ORDER-GIVING.
THE IMPORTANT THING IS THAT WE ARE ALL HERE AND ALL SAFE. BUT...
WHERE'S VAKAMA?
RIGHT HERE, SISTER. NOW ARE WE GOING TO PLAY IN THE MUD, OR ARE WE GOING TO RESCUE MATORAN?

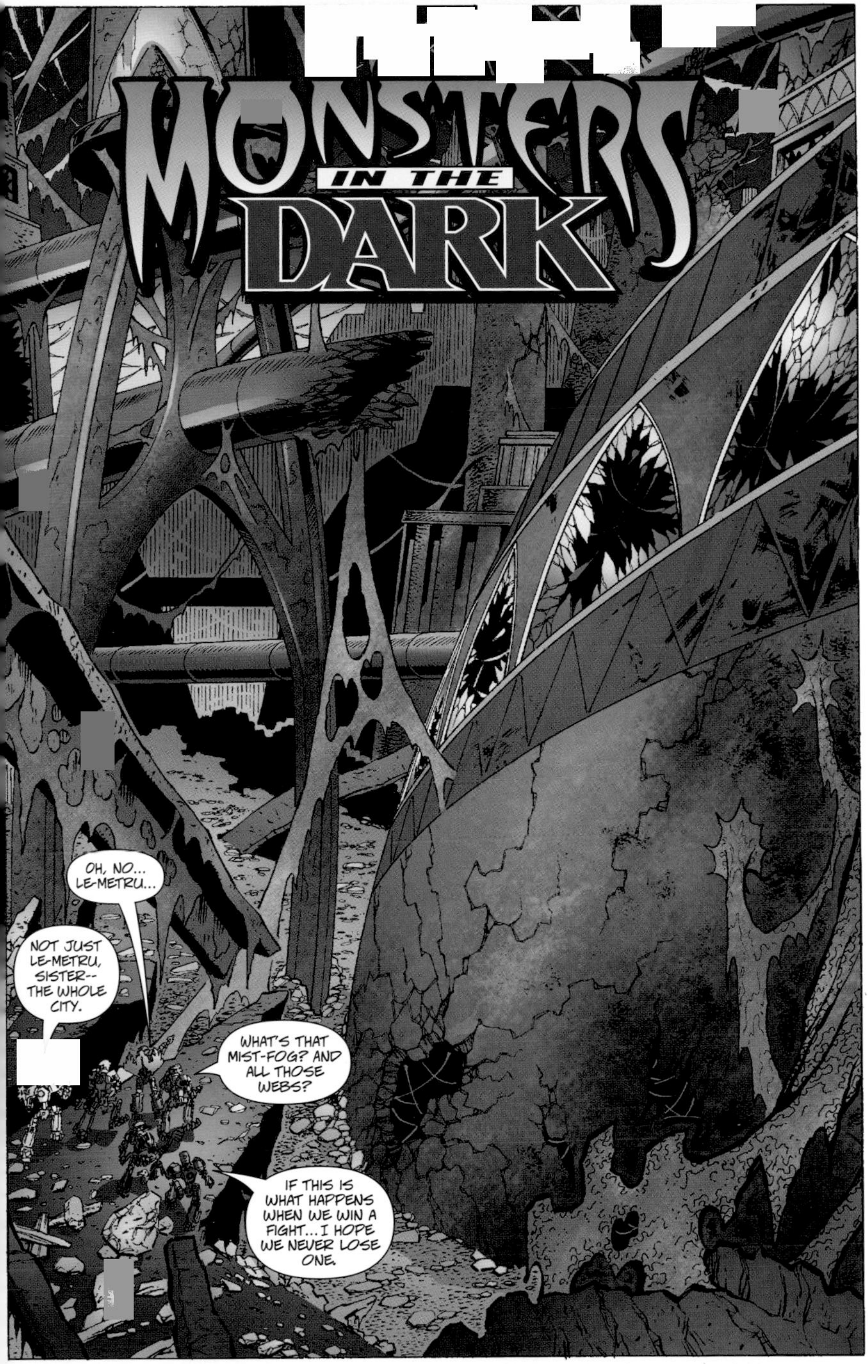
MONSTERS IN THE DARK
OH, NO... LE-METRU...
NOT JUST LE-METRU, SISTER-- THE WHOLE CITY.
WHAT'S THAT MIST-FOG? AND ALL THOSE WEBS?
IF THIS IS WHAT HAPPENS WHEN WE WIN A FIGHT... I HOPE WE NEVER LOSE ONE.

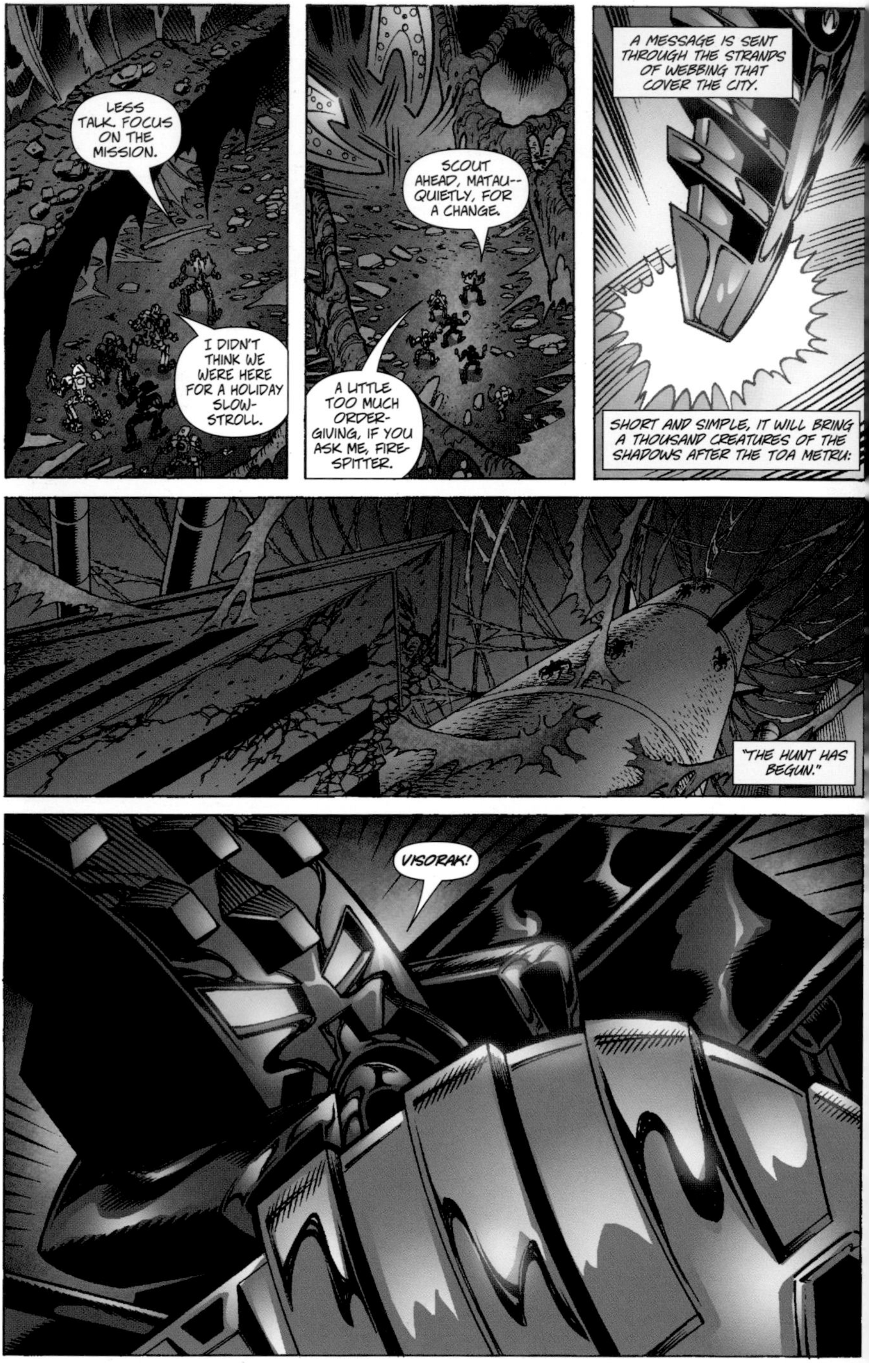
LESS TALK. FOCUS ON THE MISSION.
I DIDN'T THINK WE WERE HERE FOR A HOLIDAY SLOW-STROLL.
SCOUT AHEAD, MATAU-- QUIETLY, FOR A CHANGE.
A LITTLE TOO MUCH ORDER-GIVING, IF YOU ASK ME, FIRE-SPITTER.
A MESSAGE IS SENT THROUGH THE STRANDS OF WEBBING THAT COVER THE CITY.
SHORT AND SIMPLE, IT WILL BRING A THOUSAND CREATURES OF THE SHADOWS AFTER THE TOA METRU:
"THE HUNT HAS BEGUN."
VISORAK!

WHAT?

I DIDN'T MAKE THE CONNECTION BEFORE, BUT THE WEBS... THERE WAS A TABLET IN THE ARCHIVES THAT MENTIONED THEM. IN THEIR OWN TONGUE, THEIR NAME MEANS "STEALERS OF LIFE."

THAT NAME... ONEWA, YOU SAID THAT NAME ONCE, WHEN YOU WERE IN A TRANCE.*

*IN BIONICLE ADVENTURES #6: MAZE OF SHADOWS.

"LEGEND SAYS THEY HAVE OVERRUN HUNDREDS OF LANDS, WRAPPING THE INHABITANTS UP INSIDE WEB COCOONS.

"AND WHEN THEY EMERGE, THEY HAVE BECOME...

"WELL, YOU DON'T WANT TO KNOW WHAT THEY'VE BECOME."

ANOTHER THREAT TO THE SAFETY OF THE MATORAN. THAT'S ALL THE MORE REASON FOR US TO KEEP GOING.

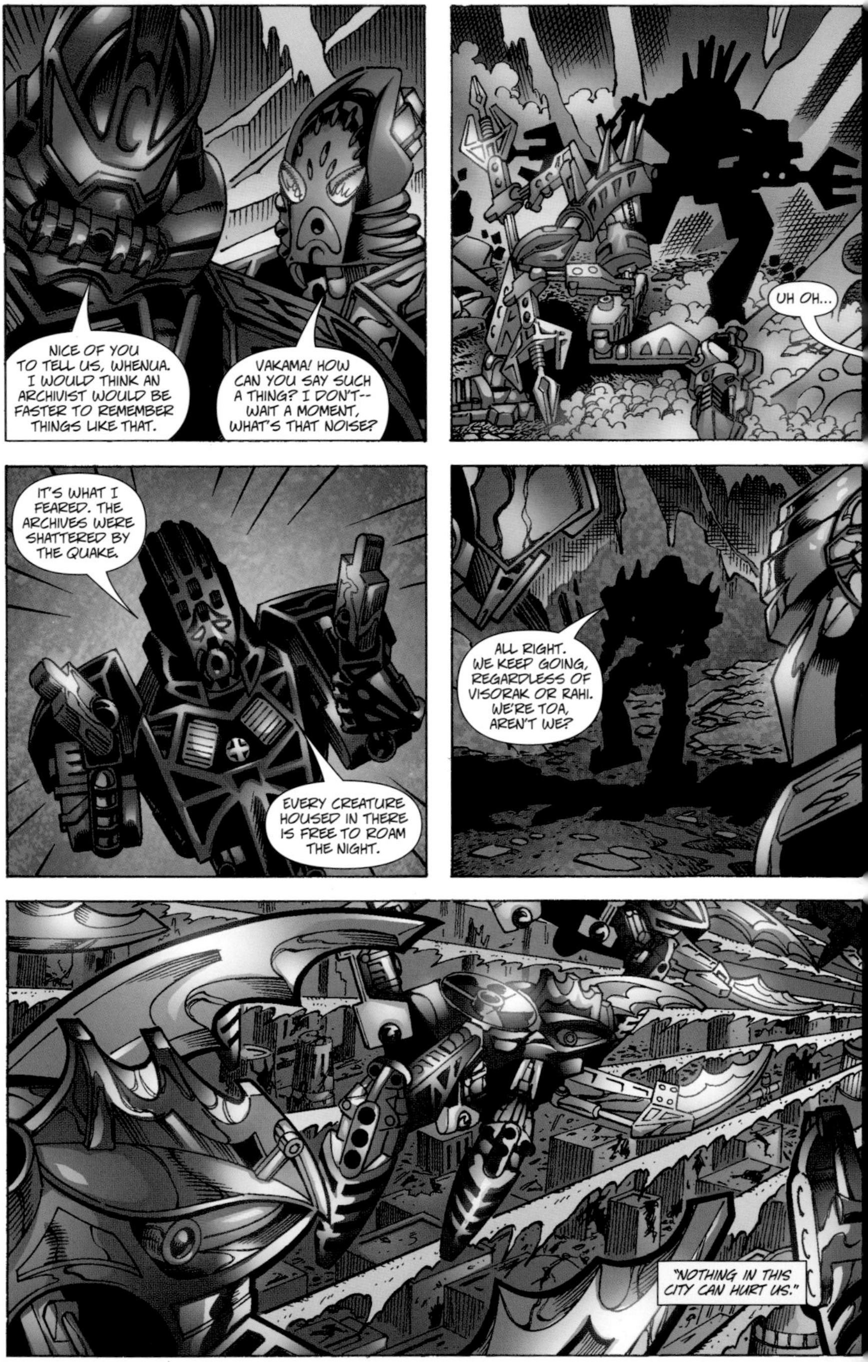
NICE OF YOU TO TELL US, WHENUA. I WOULD THINK AN ARCHIVIST WOULD BE FASTER TO REMEMBER THINGS LIKE THAT.
VAKAMA! HOW CAN YOU SAY SUCH A THING? I DON'T-- WAIT A MOMENT, WHAT'S THAT NOISE?
UH OH...
IT'S WHAT I FEARED. THE ARCHIVES WERE SHATTERED BY THE QUAKE.
EVERY CREATURE HOUSED IN THERE IS FREE TO ROAM THE NIGHT.
ALL RIGHT. WE KEEP GOING, REGARDLESS OF VISORAK OR RAHI. WE'RE TOA, AREN'T WE?
"NOTHING IN THIS CITY CAN HURT US."

LATER...

SEE? I TOLD YOU WE WOULD MAKE IT HERE WITHOUT ANY PROBLEM.

SURE, IT WAS ONE BIG HAPPY-WALK...

* FOR FULL DETAILS CHECK OUT *BIONICLE* ADVENTURES 7: *WEB OF THE VISORAK.*

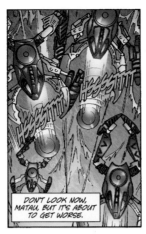

DON'T LOOK NOW, MATAU, BUT IT'S ABOUT TO GET WORSE.

THE VISORAK SPINNERS STRIKE THEIR TARGETS.

UNNNGGHH!

INSTANTLY PARALYZED, THE TOA FALL!

SENSING FINAL VICTORY, THE VISORAK KEELERAK CLOSE IN ON THE HELPLESS TOA.

THE HUNT HAS ENDED IN THE ONLY WAY IT COULD. BUT THE NIGHTMARE IS JUST BEGINNING...

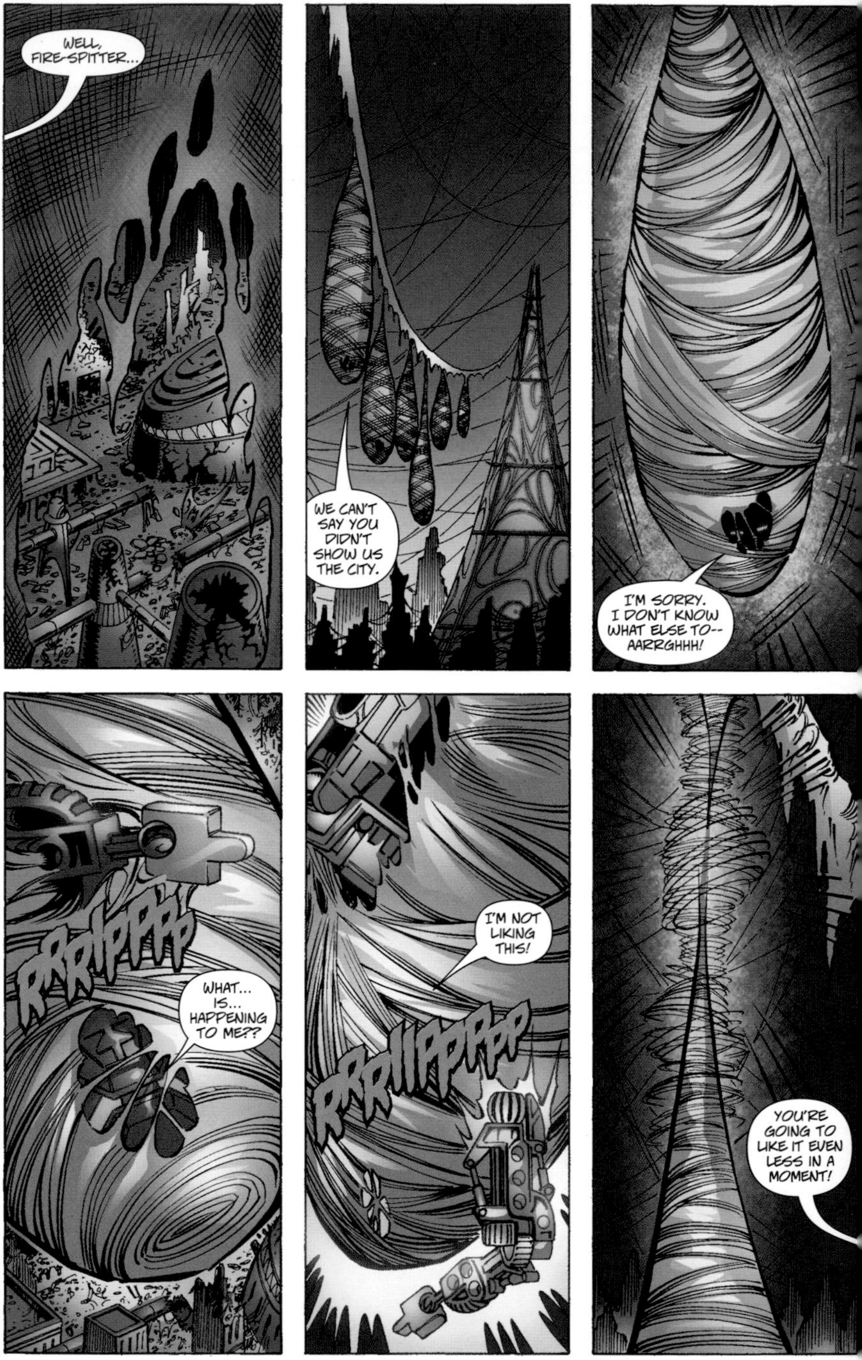
WELL, FIRE-SPITTER...
WE CAN'T SAY YOU DIDN'T SHOW US THE CITY.
I'M SORRY. I DON'T KNOW WHAT ELSE TO-- AARRGHHH!
RRRIPPP
WHAT... IS... HAPPENING TO ME??
I'M NOT LIKING THIS!
RRRIIPPPP
YOU'RE GOING TO LIKE IT EVEN LESS IN A MOMENT!

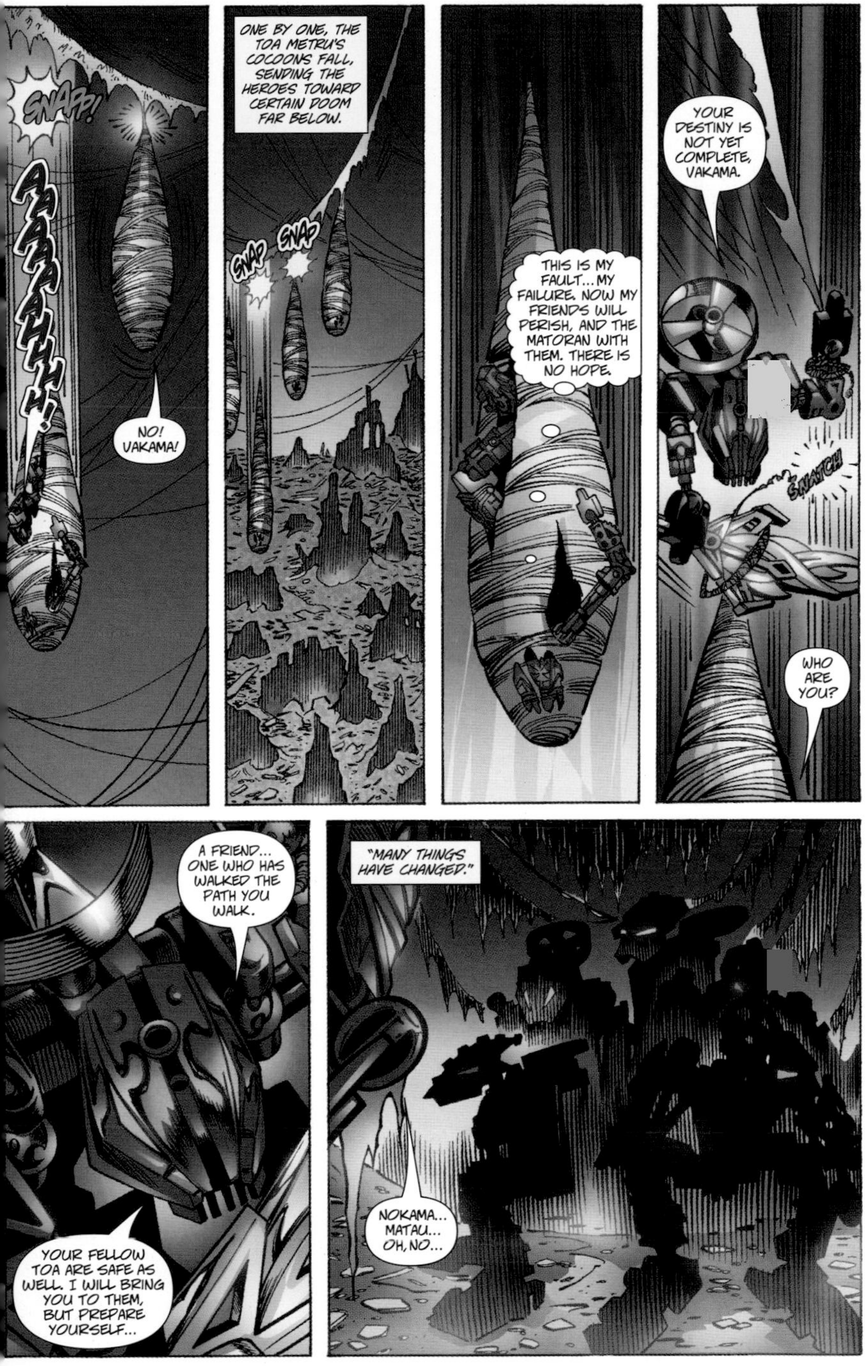
SNAPP!
NO! VAKAMA!
ONE BY ONE, THE TOA METRU'S COCOONS FALL, SENDING THE HEROES TOWARD CERTAIN DOOM FAR BELOW.
SNAP
SNAP
THIS IS MY FAULT... MY FAILURE. NOW MY FRIENDS WILL PERISH, AND THE MATORAN WITH THEM. THERE IS NO HOPE.
YOUR DESTINY IS NOT YET COMPLETE, VAKAMA.
SNATCH
WHO ARE YOU?
A FRIEND... ONE WHO HAS WALKED THE PATH YOU WALK.
YOUR FELLOW TOA ARE SAFE AS WELL. I WILL BRING YOU TO THEM, BUT PREPARE YOURSELF...
"MANY THINGS HAVE CHANGED."
NOKAMA... MATAU... OH, NO...

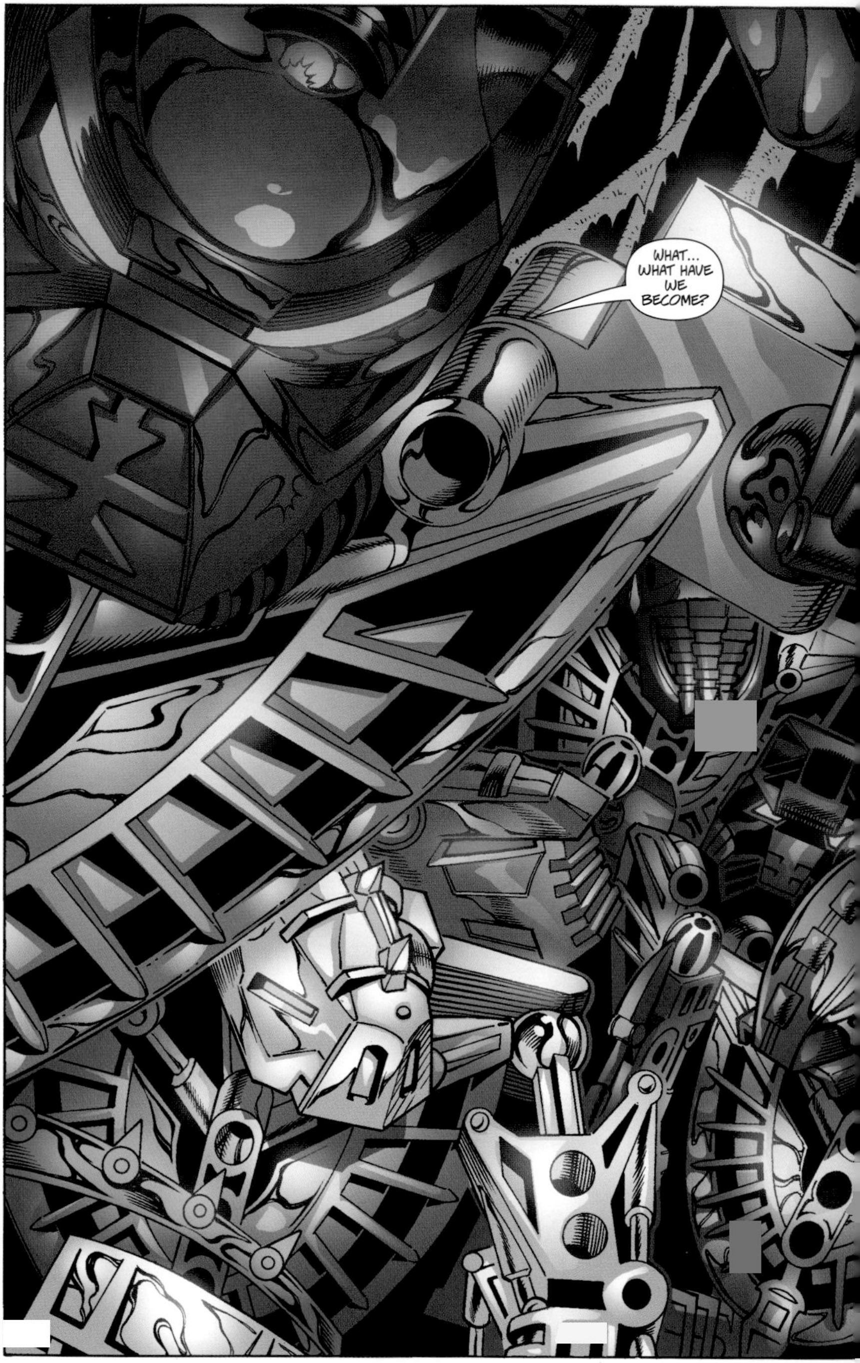
WHAT... WHAT HAVE WE BECOME?

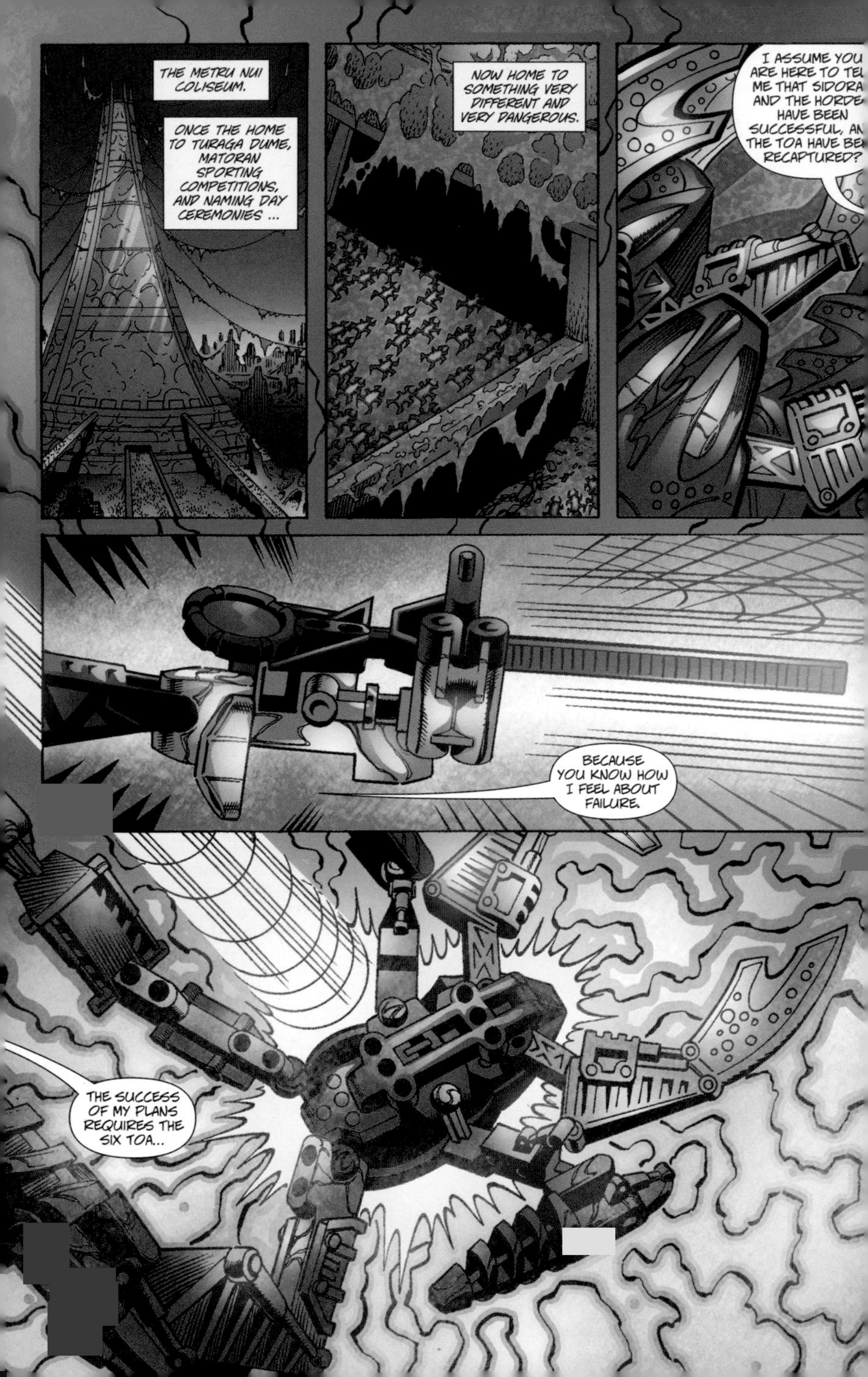
THE METRU NUI COLISEUM.
ONCE THE HOME TO TURAGA DUME, MATORAN SPORTING COMPETITIONS, AND NAMING DAY CEREMONIES ...
NOW HOME TO SOMETHING VERY DIFFERENT AND VERY DANGEROUS.
I ASSUME YOU ARE HERE TO TEL ME THAT SIDORA AND THE HORDE HAVE BEEN SUCCESSFUL, AN THE TOA HAVE BEE RECAPTURED?
BECAUSE YOU KNOW HOW I FEEL ABOUT FAILURE.
THE SUCCESS OF MY PLANS REQUIRES THE SIX TOA...

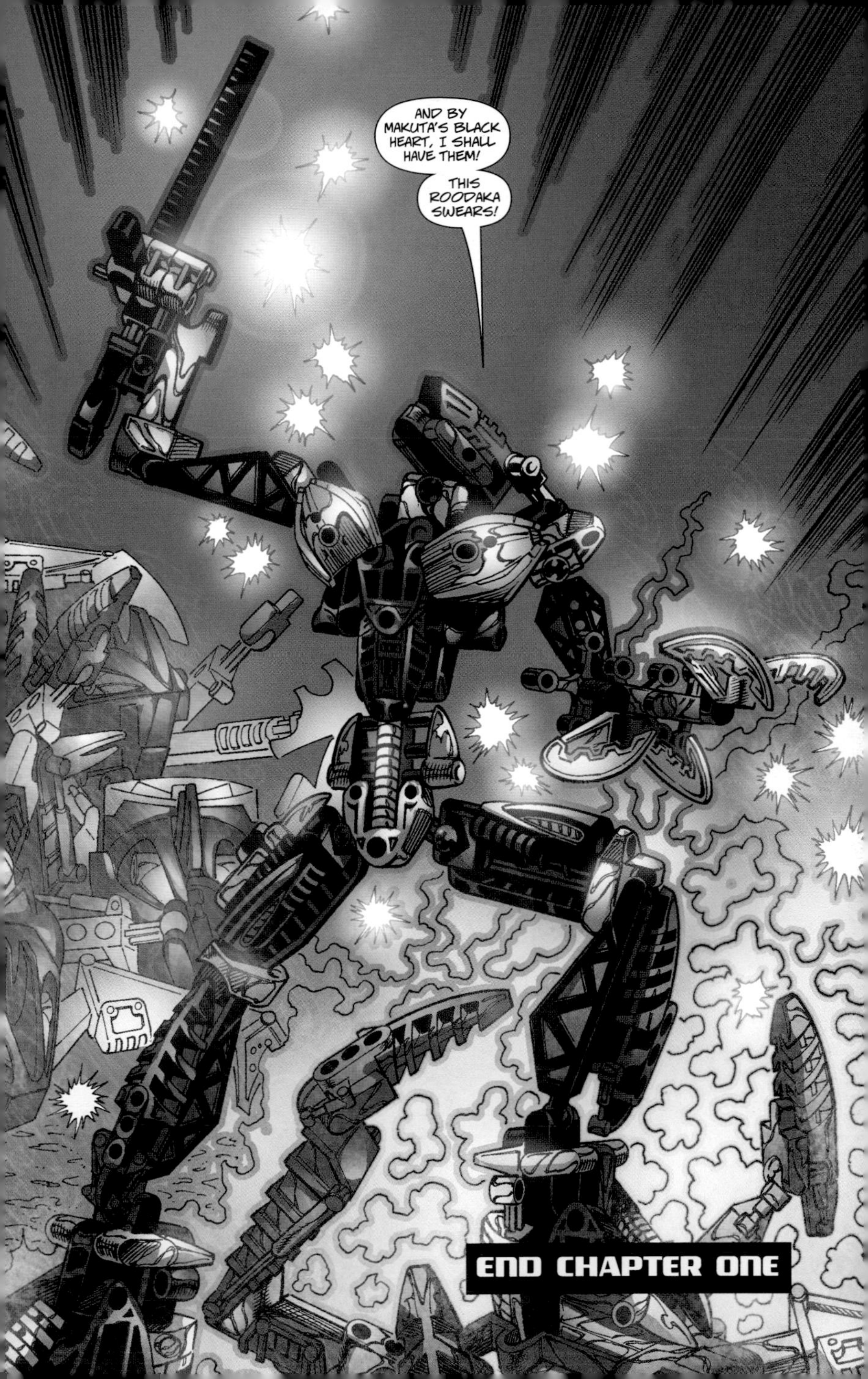
AND BY MAKUTA'S BLACK HEART, I SHALL HAVE THEM!
THIS ROODAKA SWEARS!
END CHAPTER ONE

CHAPTER TWO

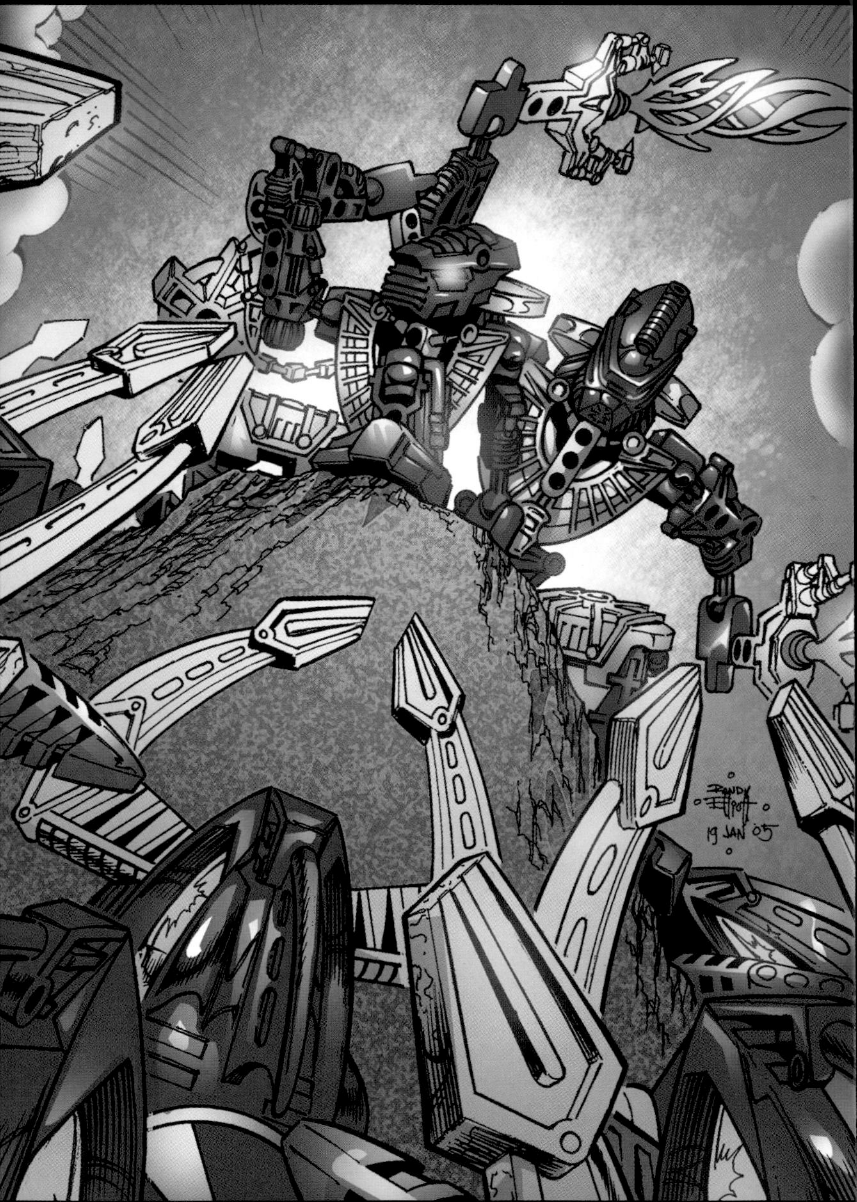
19 JAN '05

PO-METRU.

A SMALL HERD OF KIKANALO PAUSES TO GRAZE ON THE SPARSE VEGETATION OF A CANYON. IT IS A PEACEFUL MOMENT.

ONE THAT CAN'T LAST.

HSsssft

DISRUPTER SPINNERS WEAKEN THE RAHI AND BRING THEM DOWN.

THE VISORAK ROPORAK MOVE IN TO FINISH THEIR TASK, WEBBING THE KIKANALO UP. SOME WILL BE IMPRISONED IN COCOONS, OTHERS MUTATED, WITH NO CHANCE TO ASK ...

WHY??? WHY HARM RAHI THAT ARE NO THREAT TO THEM?

IT IS THE VISORAK'S WAY. ANYTHING THAT MOVES, ANYTHING THAT LIVES MUST BE MADE SILENT AND STILL.

I HAVE SEEN THIS REPEATED DOZENS OF TIMES. THE VISORAK HORDES COME, CONQUER, AND LEAVE A DEAD LAND BEHIND.

NOT THIS TIME. NOT IN MY CITY.

VAKAMA! THIS WAS JUST MEANT TO BE A SCOUTING MISSION!

HE'S NOT LISTENING, RAHAGA. THEN AGAIN, WHEN DOES HE EVER?

YOU ARE THE ONE WHO SHOWED ME HOW TO CHARGE THIS RHOTUKA SPINNER WITH MY NEW TOOLS, NORIK.

NOW SHUT UP AND LET ME DO MY JOB!

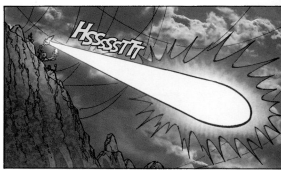

HSSSSTTT

VENGEANCE OF THE VISORAK

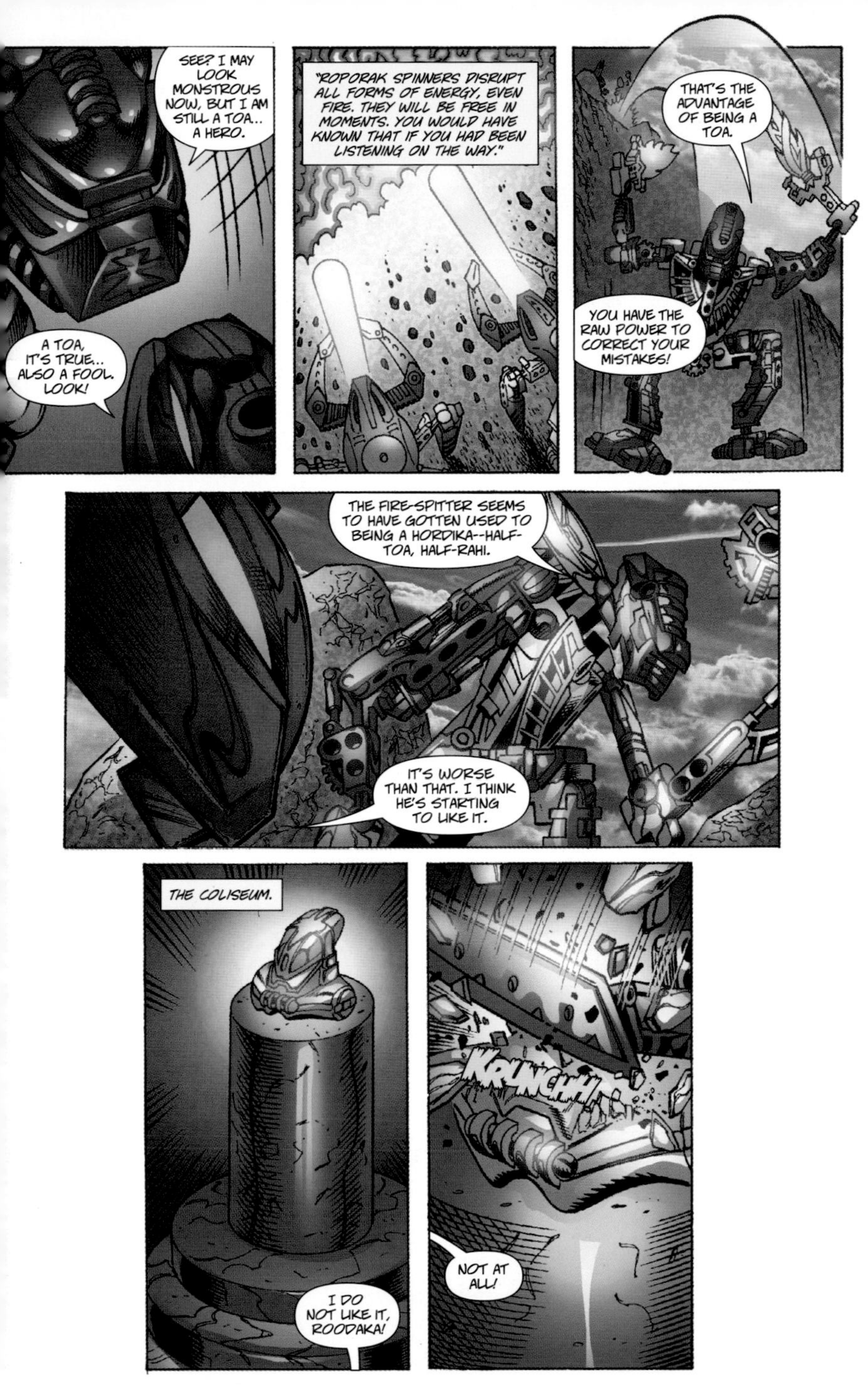
SEE? I MAY LOOK MONSTROUS NOW, BUT I AM STILL A TOA... A HERO.
A TOA, IT'S TRUE... ALSO A FOOL. LOOK!
"ROPORAK SPINNERS DISRUPT ALL FORMS OF ENERGY, EVEN FIRE. THEY WILL BE FREE IN MOMENTS. YOU WOULD HAVE KNOWN THAT IF YOU HAD BEEN LISTENING ON THE WAY."
THAT'S THE ADVANTAGE OF BEING A TOA.
YOU HAVE THE RAW POWER TO CORRECT YOUR MISTAKES!
THE FIRE-SPITTER SEEMS TO HAVE GOTTEN USED TO BEING A HORDIKA--HALF-TOA, HALF-RAHI.
IT'S WORSE THAN THAT. I THINK HE'S STARTING TO LIKE IT.
THE COLISEUM.
I DO NOT LIKE IT, ROODAKA!
KRUNCHH!
NOT AT ALL!

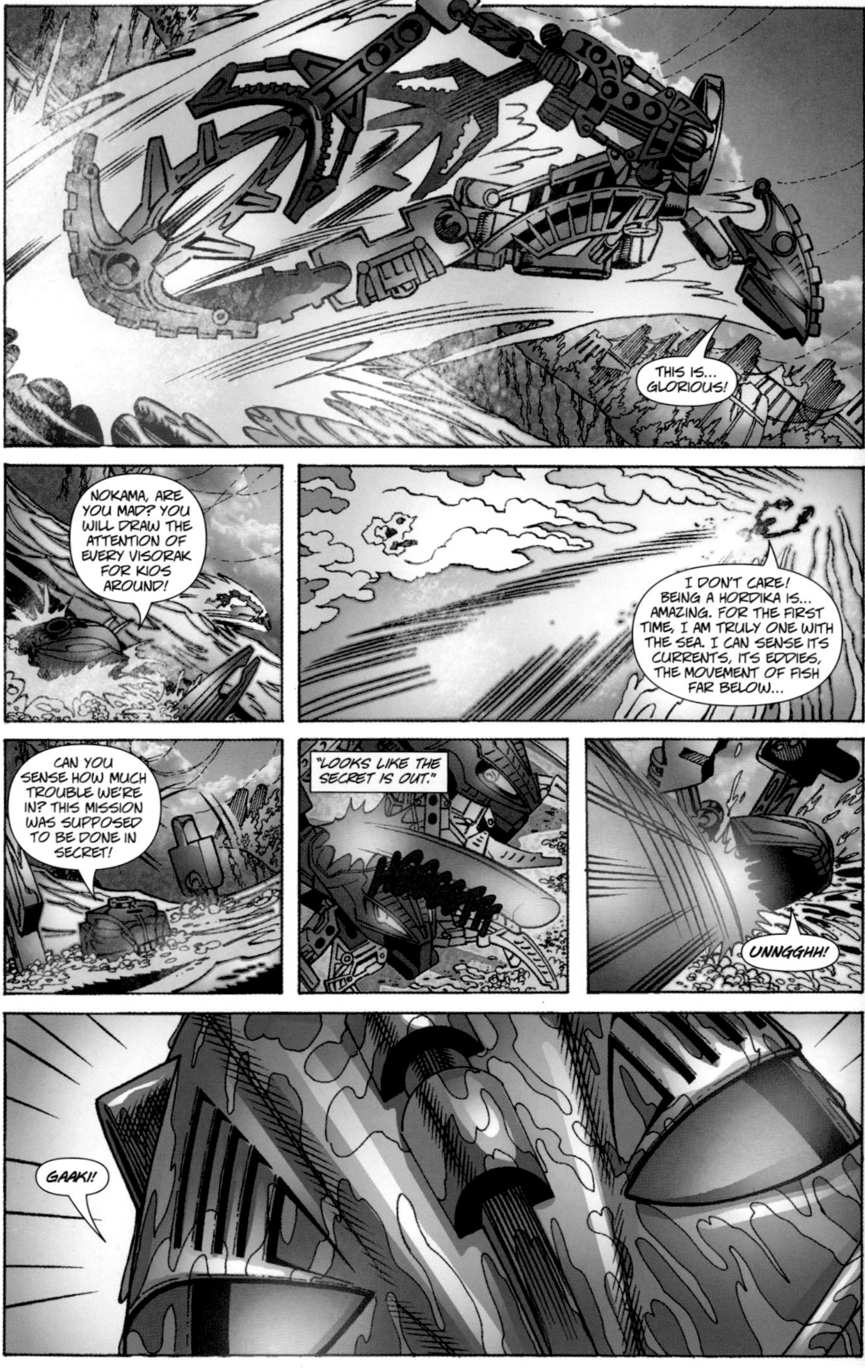

THIS IS... GLORIOUS!
NOKAMA, ARE YOU MAD? YOU WILL DRAW THE ATTENTION OF EVERY VISORAK FOR KIOS AROUND!
I DON'T CARE! BEING A HORDIKA IS... AMAZING. FOR THE FIRST TIME, I AM TRULY ONE WITH THE SEA. I CAN SENSE ITS CURRENTS, ITS EDDIES, THE MOVEMENT OF FISH FAR BELOW...
CAN YOU SENSE HOW MUCH TROUBLE WE'RE IN? THIS MISSION WAS SUPPOSED TO BE DONE IN SECRET!
"LOOKS LIKE THE SECRET IS OUT."
UNNGGHH!
GAAKI!

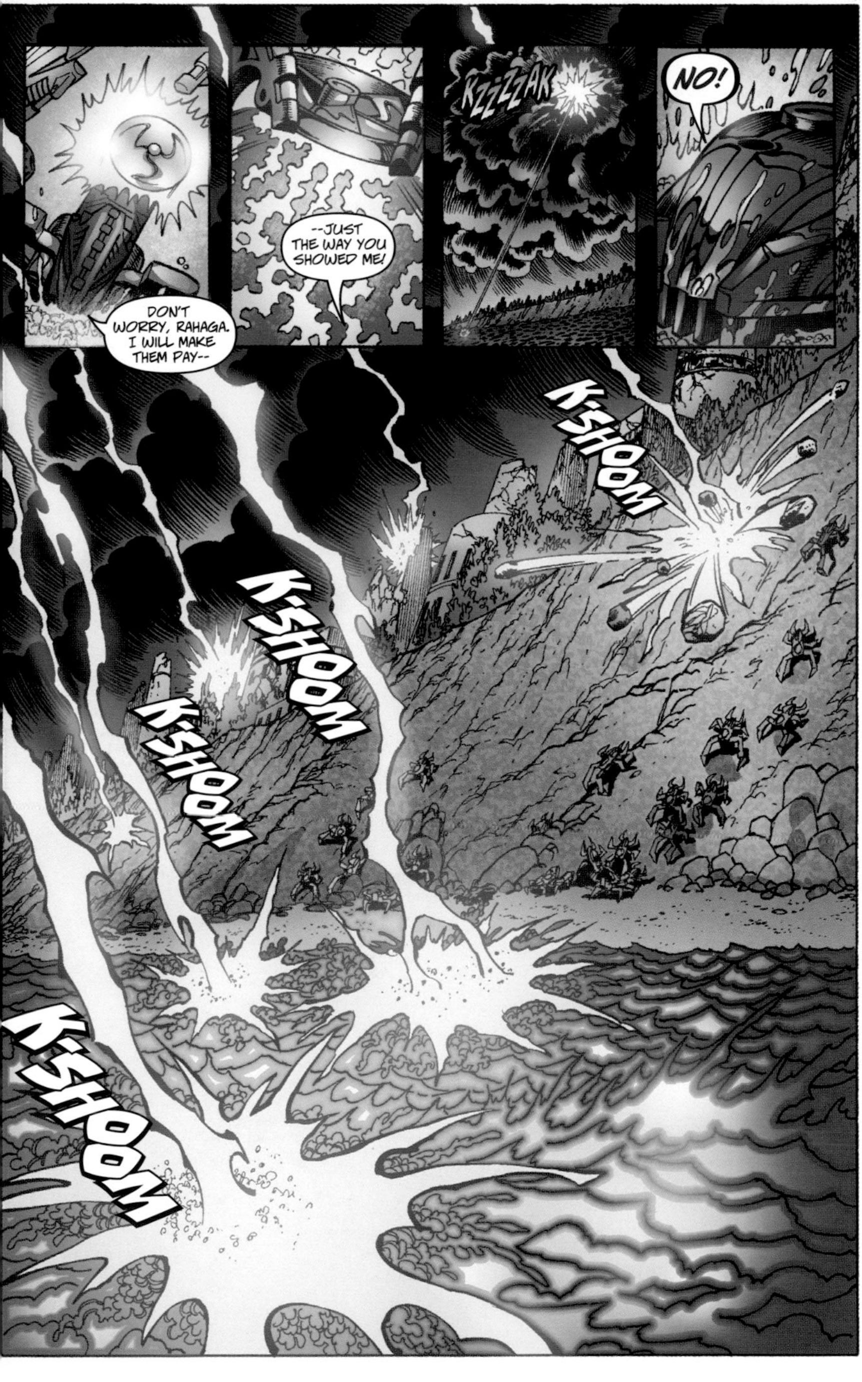
DON'T WORRY, RAHAGA. I WILL MAKE THEM PAY--
--JUST THE WAY YOU SHOWED ME!
KZZZZAK
NO!
K-SHOOM
K-SHOOM
K-SHOOM
K-SHOOM

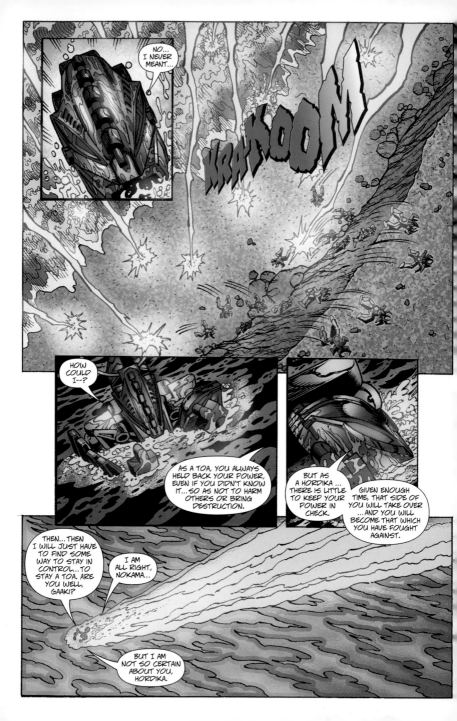

KO-METRU.

CLICK-CLICK... WHEET... CLICK... WHEET-WHEET.

WHAT IN MATA NUI'S NAME ARE YOU DOING?

TALKING TO THOSE RAHI UP THERE. YOU MIGHT WANT TO TRY IT SOMETIME.

I HAVE NOTHING TO LEARN FROM BIRDS.

THEY ARE FLYING FREE UP THERE.

YOU ARE DOWN HERE, MUTATED INTO A TOA HORDIKA AND ON THE RUN FROM THE VISORAK HORDE.

MAYBE IT IS THEM WHO HAVE NOTHING TO LEARN FROM YOU, NUJU.

"YOU ARE VERY WISE, TOA, BUT IN THIS NEW WORLD, WISDOM IS NOT ENOUGH."

THEIR TONE IS ANGRY. NOW IS THE TIME TO STRIKE.*

TOO SIMPLE. NOTHING IN THIS CITY IS WORTH HUNTING. SIDORAK PROMISED US GOOD SPORT, REMEMBER?

I REMEMBER. I REMEMBER WHAT ROODAKA DID TO THE LAST ONE WHO COMPLAINED, TOO.

*TRANSLATED FROM VISORAK

OOHNORAK CAN IMITATE THE VOICES OF THOSE YOU TRUST, STOLEN FROM YOUR VERY THOUGHTS. I TRIED TO WARN YOU!

NEXT TIME, TRY HARDER!

I ENDURED YOUR VENOM, CREATURE ... AND YOUR WEBS ... BUT ONE THING I WILL NOT ENDURE--

--IS YOUR BREATH!

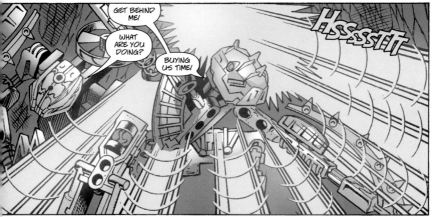

GET BEHIND ME!

WHAT ARE YOU DOING?

BUYING US TIME!

HSSSSSTT

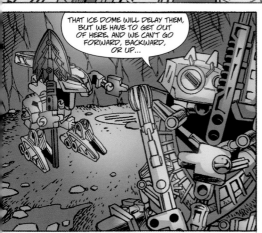

THAT ICE DOME WILL DELAY THEM, BUT WE HAVE TO GET OUT OF HERE. AND WE CAN'T GO FORWARD, BACKWARD, OR UP...

...SO WE GO DOWN.

END CHAPTER TWO

METRU NUI has changed greatly since the events of **BIONICLE 2**: *Legends of Metru Nui*. Here is a quick guide to the earthquake ravaged "city of shadows"

Po-Metru
Rockslides have blocked some canyons and passes. Previously hidden sites have been revealed, like a secret lair of Makuta.

Onu-Metru
The Archives have shattered, releasing Rahi of all sorts to roam the streets in the darkness.

Ko-Metru
Knowledge Towers suffered great damage, and fractured canals have resulted in icy pools and pillars of frozen protodermis.

Ga-Metru
Dangerous aquatic Rahi infest the waterways, while protodermis experiments have leaked out of the damaged schools.

Ta-Metru
Molten protodermis has flooded some areas, while shattered foundries fill the metru with fire and smoke.

Le-Metru
Now a dangerous, mechanized jungle, Le-Metru is home to many of the wild Rahi who have escaped the Archives.

TRIAL BY FIRE
CHAPTER THREE

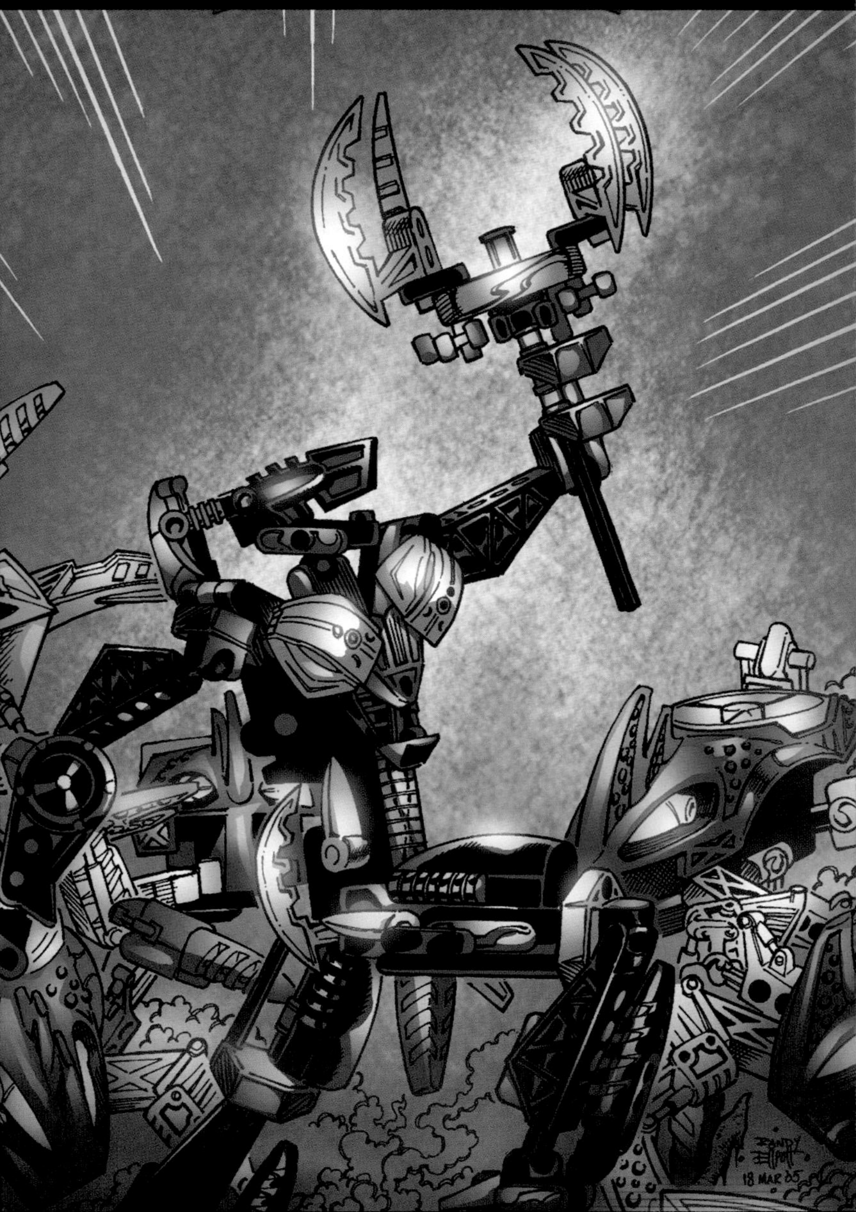

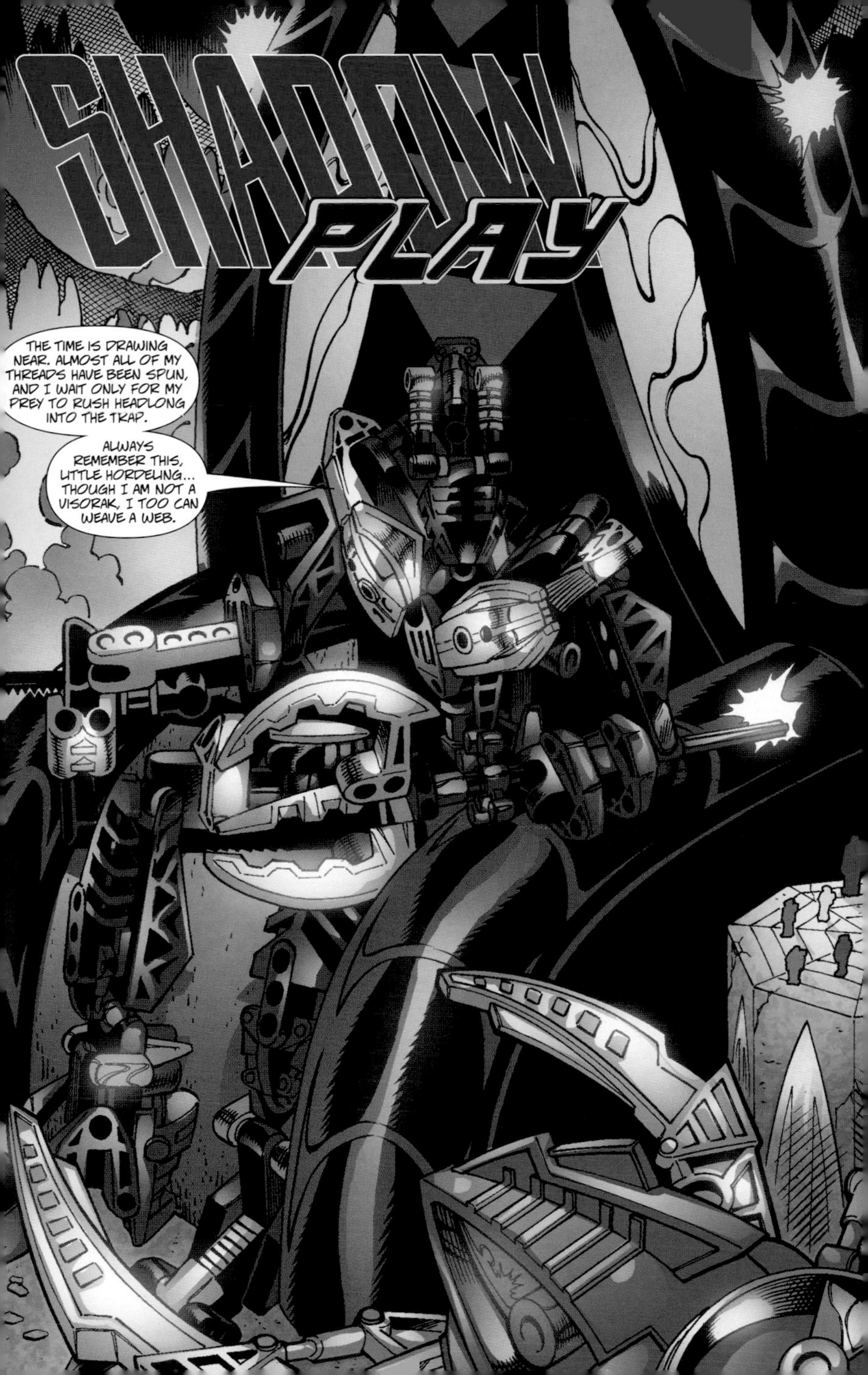
SHADOW PLAY
THE TIME IS DRAWING NEAR. ALMOST ALL OF MY THREADS HAVE BEEN SPUN, AND I WAIT ONLY FOR MY PREY TO RUSH HEADLONG INTO THE TRAP.
ALWAYS REMEMBER THIS, LITTLE HORDELING... THOUGH I AM NOT A VISORAK, I TOO CAN WEAVE A WEB.

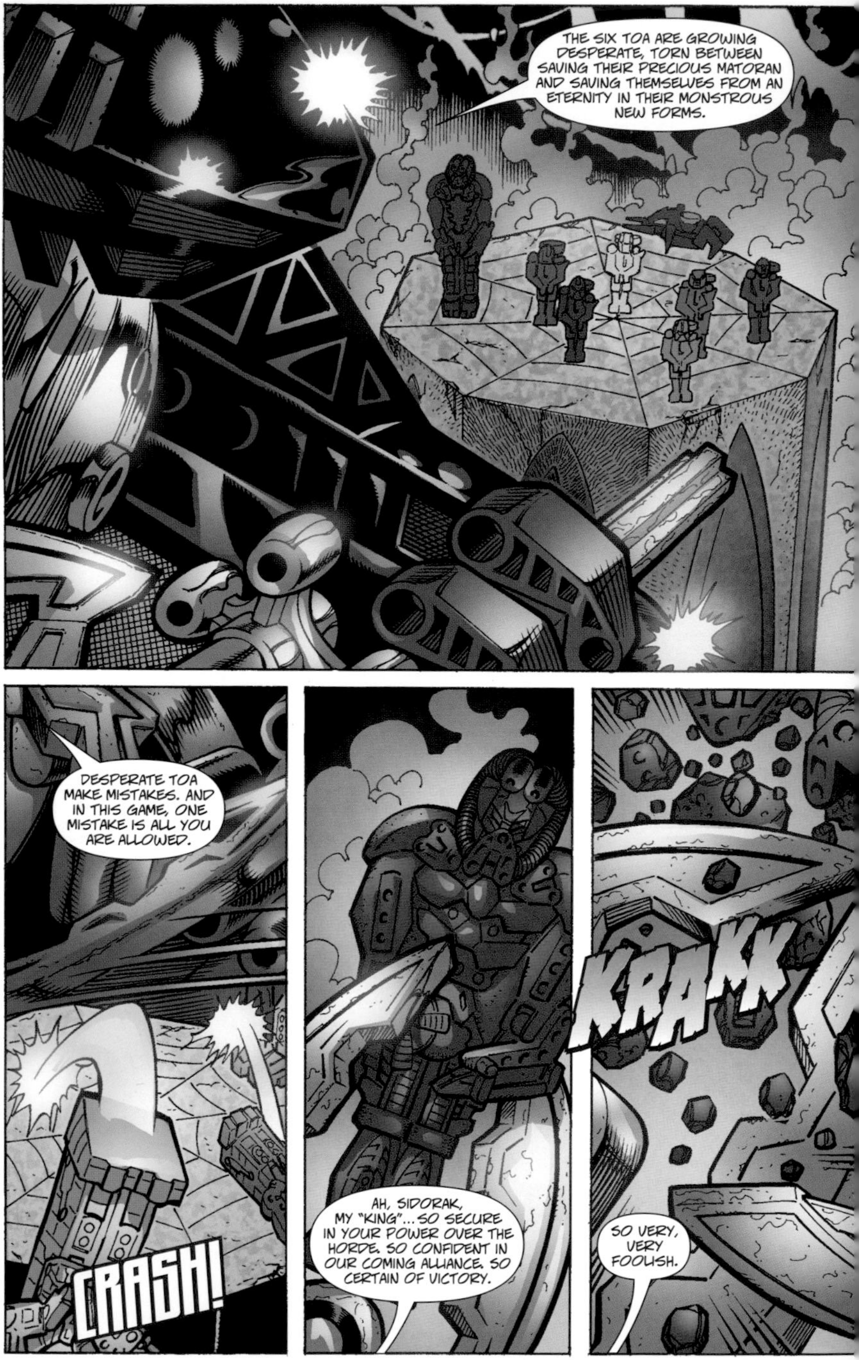
THE SIX TOA ARE GROWING DESPERATE, TORN BETWEEN SAVING THEIR PRECIOUS MATORAN AND SAVING THEMSELVES FROM AN ETERNITY IN THEIR MONSTROUS NEW FORMS.
DESPERATE TOA MAKE MISTAKES. AND IN THIS GAME, ONE MISTAKE IS ALL YOU ARE ALLOWED.
CRASH!
AH, SIDORAK, MY "KING"... SO SECURE IN YOUR POWER OVER THE HORDE. SO CONFIDENT IN OUR COMING ALLIANCE. SO CERTAIN OF VICTORY.
KRAKK
SO VERY, VERY FOOLISH.

WHERE I COME FROM, HORDELING, THERE IS A RITE OF PASSAGE--A MOUNTAIN THAT TWO CLIMB TOGETHER.

THE SKY RAINS FIRE... THE GRASSES ARE FILLED WITH ACID... AND THE ROCK ITSELF TRIES TO DEVOUR YOU AS YOU SCALE ITS SLOPES.

"ALMOST TO THE SUMMIT, MY COMPANION CRIED OUT. HIS FOOT WAS CAUGHT IN A CREVICE. THE MOUNTAIN KNEW HE WAS THERE.

ROODAKA! HELP!

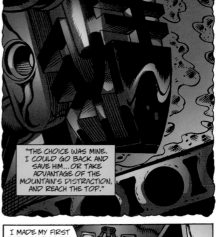

"THE CHOICE WAS MINE. I COULD GO BACK AND SAVE HIM... OR TAKE ADVANTAGE OF THE MOUNTAIN'S DISTRACTION, AND REACH THE TOP."

I MADE MY FIRST BARGAIN THAT DAY, HORDELING. I SCALED THE ROCK IN SAFETY... AND THE MOUNTAIN ENJOYED ITS FEAST.

WHICH TOA DO YOU THINK WILL MAKE A SIMILAR BARGAIN TO SAVE THEIR INSIGNIFICANT LITTLE LIFE?

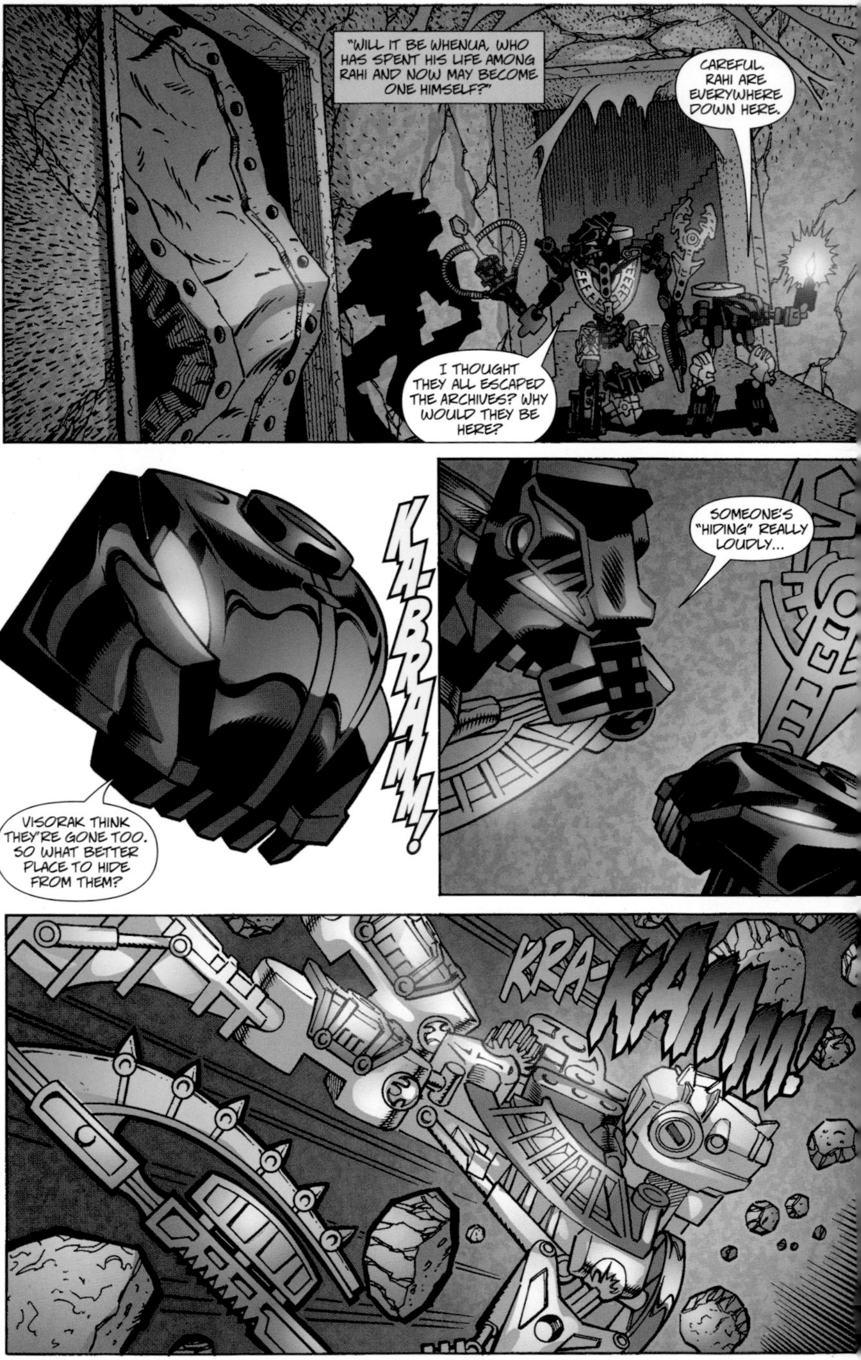
"WILL IT BE WHENUA, WHO HAS SPENT HIS LIFE AMONG RAHI AND NOW MAY BECOME ONE HIMSELF?"
CAREFUL. RAHI ARE EVERYWHERE DOWN HERE.
I THOUGHT THEY ALL ESCAPED THE ARCHIVES? WHY WOULD THEY BE HERE?
VISORAK THINK THEY'RE GONE TOO. SO WHAT BETTER PLACE TO HIDE FROM THEM?
KA-BRAMMM!
SOMEONE'S "HIDING" REALLY LOUDLY...
KRA-KAMMM!

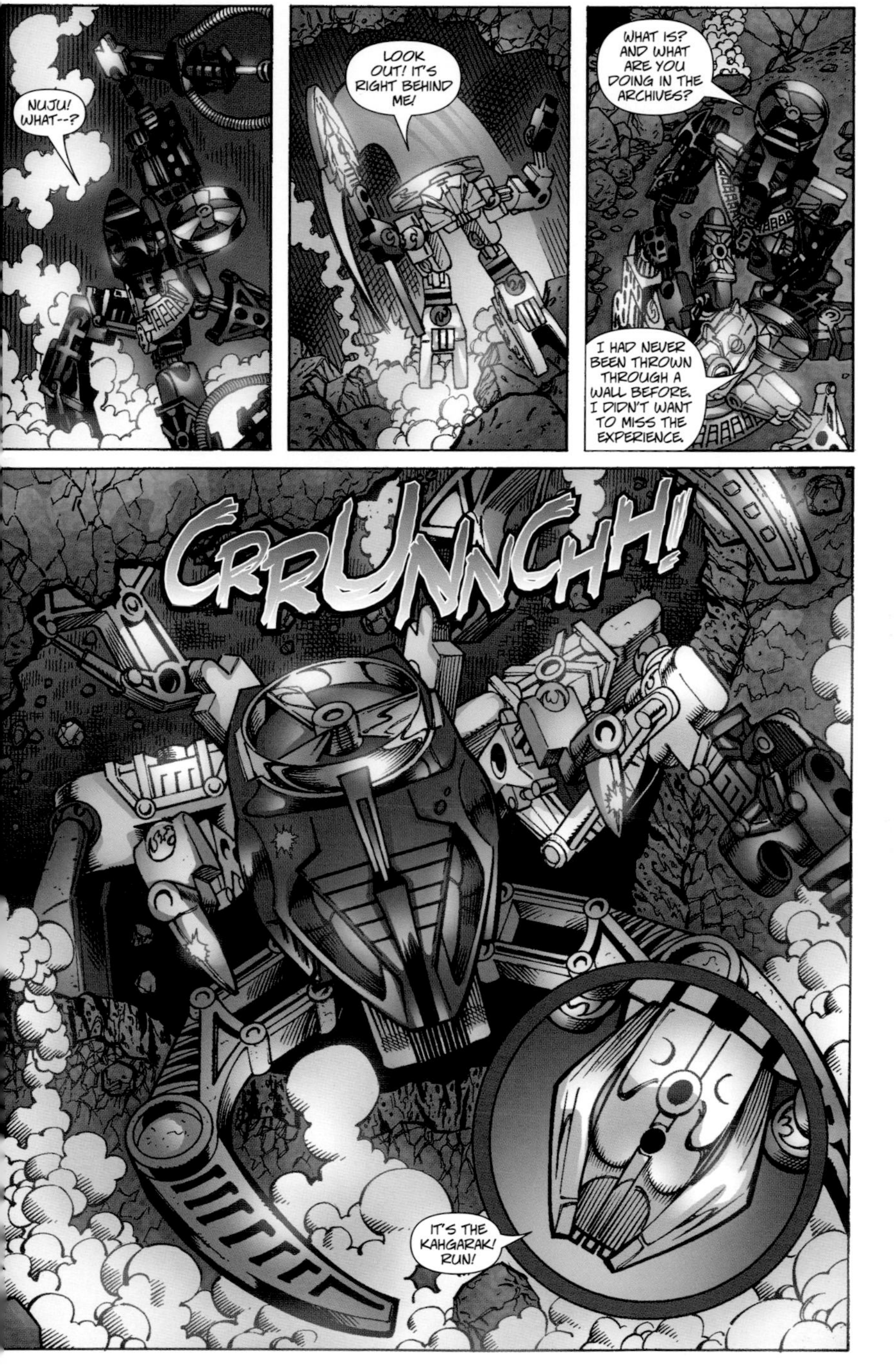
NUJU! WHAT--?
LOOK OUT! IT'S RIGHT BEHIND ME!
WHAT IS? AND WHAT ARE YOU DOING IN THE ARCHIVES?
I HAD NEVER BEEN THROWN THROUGH A WALL BEFORE. I DIDN'T WANT TO MISS THE EXPERIENCE.
CRRUNNCHH!
IT'S THE KAHGARAK! RUN!

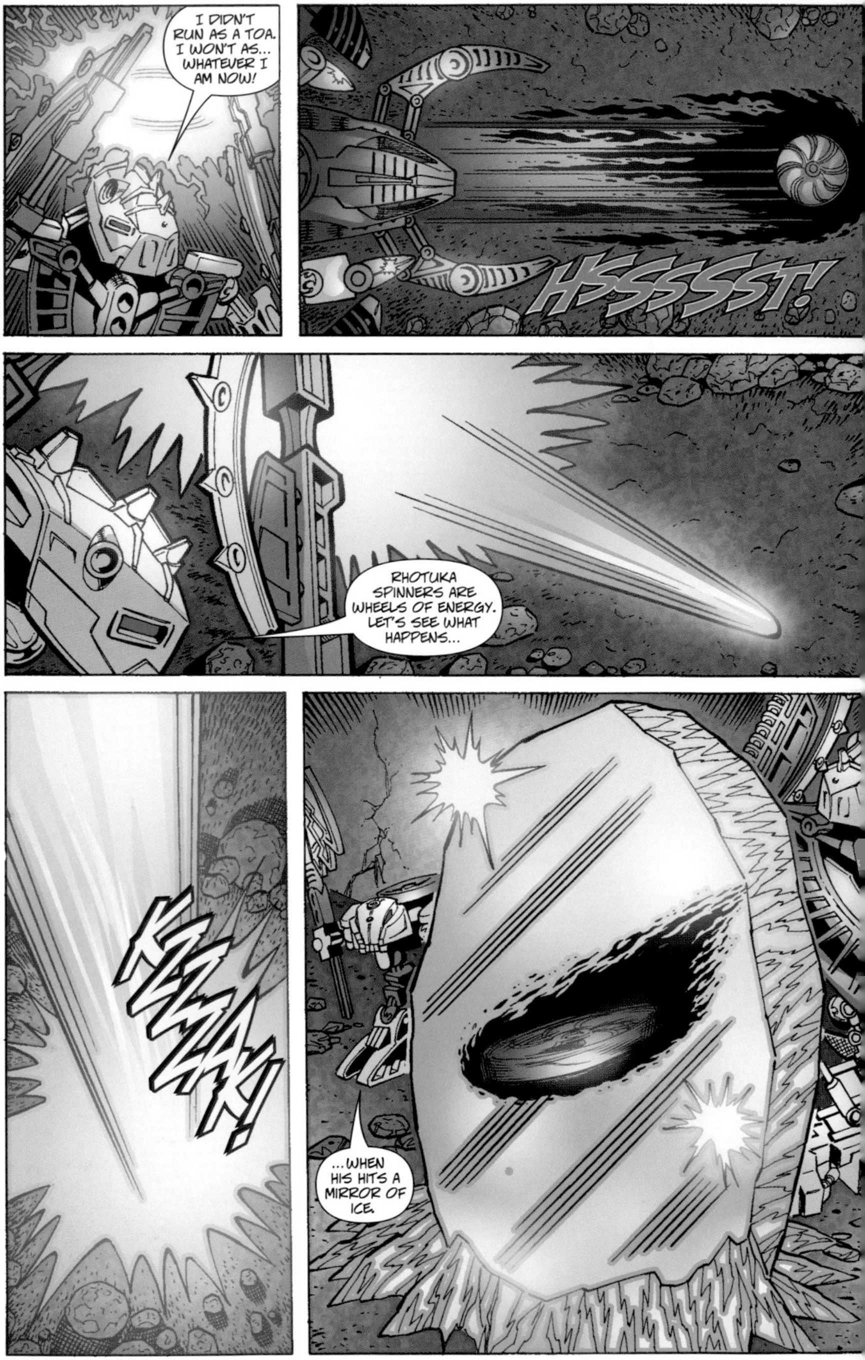
I DIDN'T RUN AS A TOA. I WON'T AS... WHATEVER I AM NOW!
HSSSSST!
RHOTUKA SPINNERS ARE WHEELS OF ENERGY. LET'S SEE WHAT HAPPENS...
KRAK!
...WHEN HIS HITS A MIRROR OF ICE.

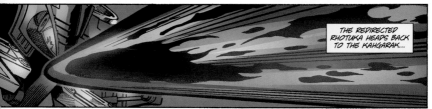

IT RECEIVED THE FATE IT PLANNED FOR YOU--TRAPPED IN SHADOW.

WHENUA LEAPS THE WAY DEEPER INTO THE ARCHIVES.

LOCK THE DOOR, NUJU. WE CAN PLAN HERE.

BUT IT WON'T STAY THERE LONG. WE HAVE TO MOVE!

BUT FIRST, I THINK WE NEED SOME ANSWERS. WHAT ARE THE VISORAK? WHY ARE THEY HERE?

I CAN ANSWER THAT... OH, YES... FOR I WAS ONE OF THE FIRST TO SEE THEM, AND SURVIVE.

"THEY FIRST APPEARED YEARS AGO... SAVAGE BY NATURE, OBEDIENT BY TRAINING. NOTHING THAT LIVED COULD STAND BEFORE THEM.

"AT FIRST, I THOUGHT THE VISORAK WERE THE ONLY DANGER... UNTIL I SAW THEM. ROODAKA AND SIDORAK

THAT WAS WHEN I KNEW WHO WAS REALLY BEHIND THIS. AND IT WASN'T SIDORAK, OR HIS FOUL VICEROY. IT WAS THE ---

LOOK OUT!

KRUNNCH

KRRUNNCH

SMACK

THEY'RE COMING THROUGH THE VENTILATION SYSTEM!

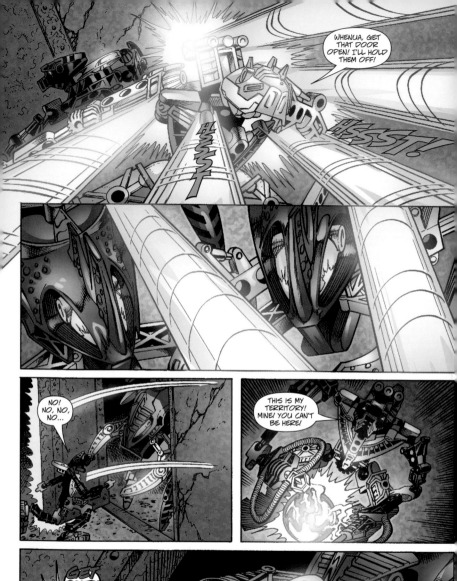

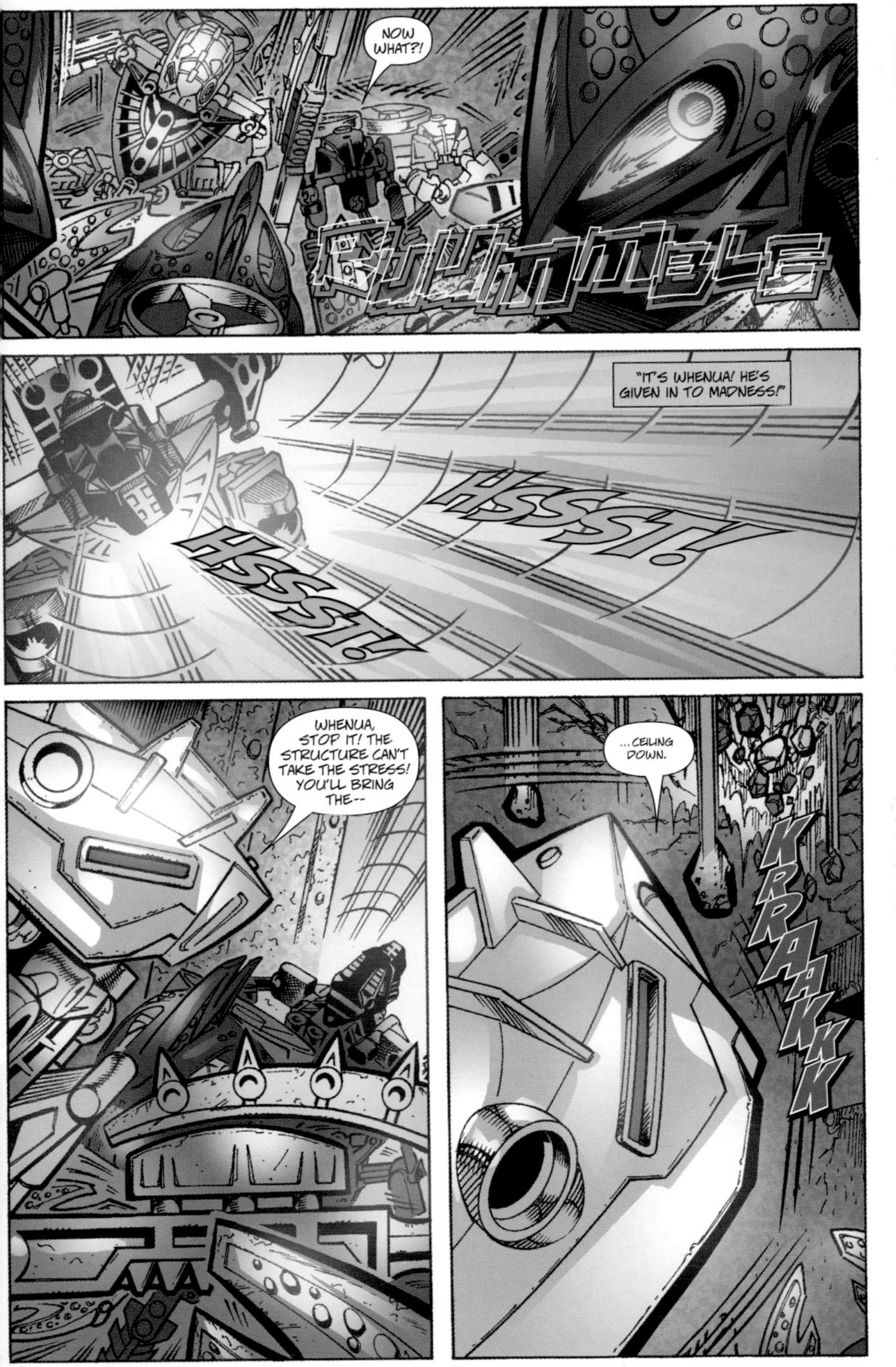
NOW WHAT?!
"IT'S WHENUA! HE'S GIVEN IN TO MADNESS!"
HSSST!
HSSST!
WHENUA, STOP IT! THE STRUCTURE CAN'T TAKE THE STRESS! YOU'LL BRING THE--
...CEILING DOWN.
KRRAAKKK

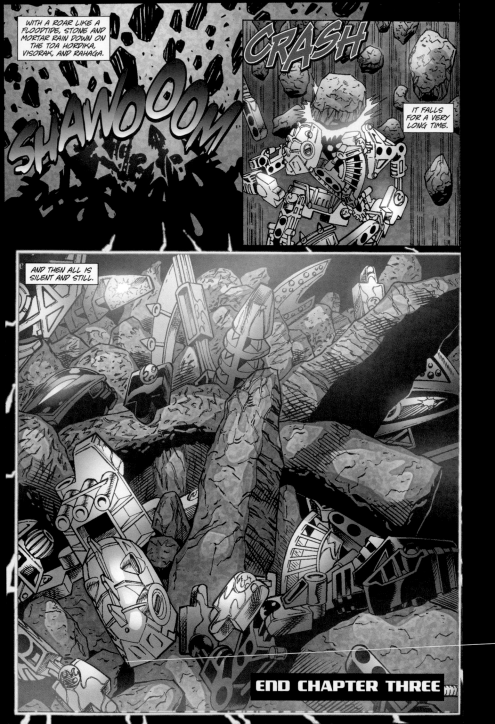

TRIAL BY FIRE
CHAPTER FOUR

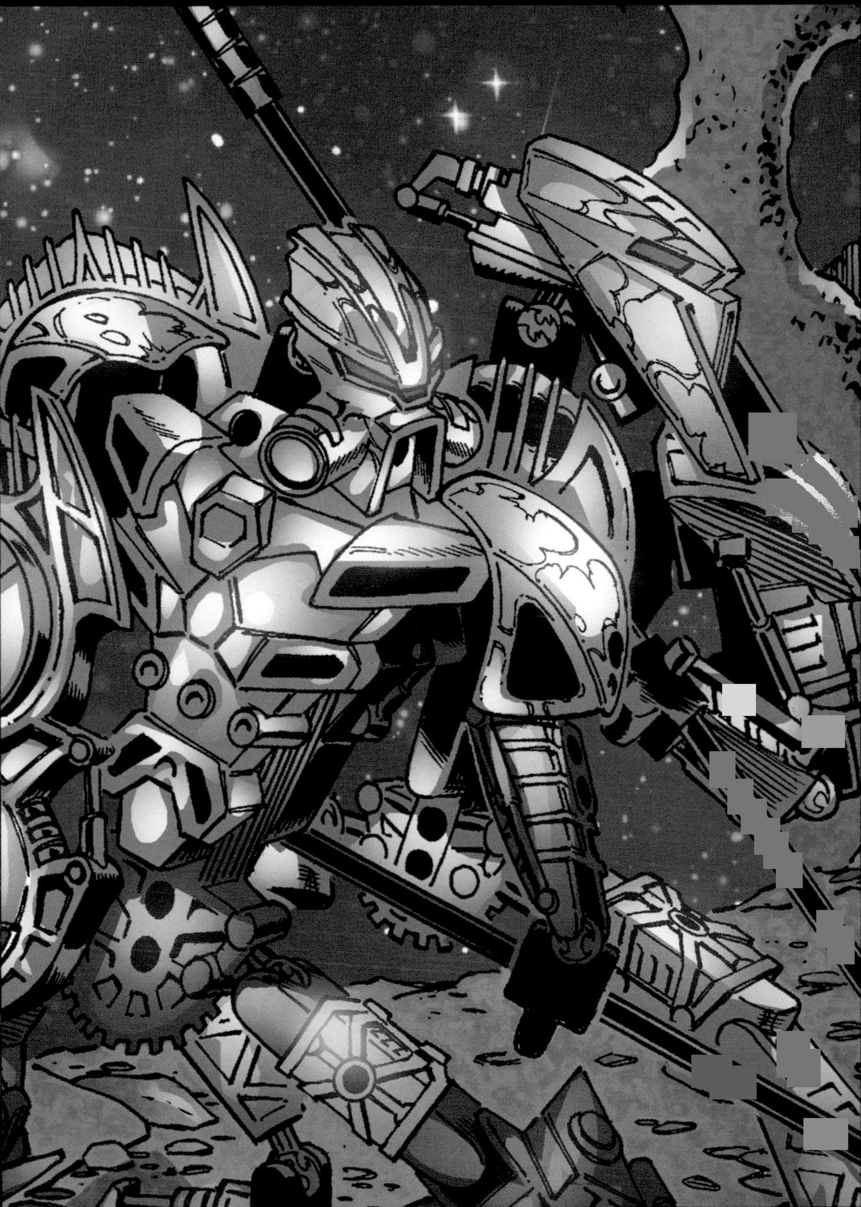

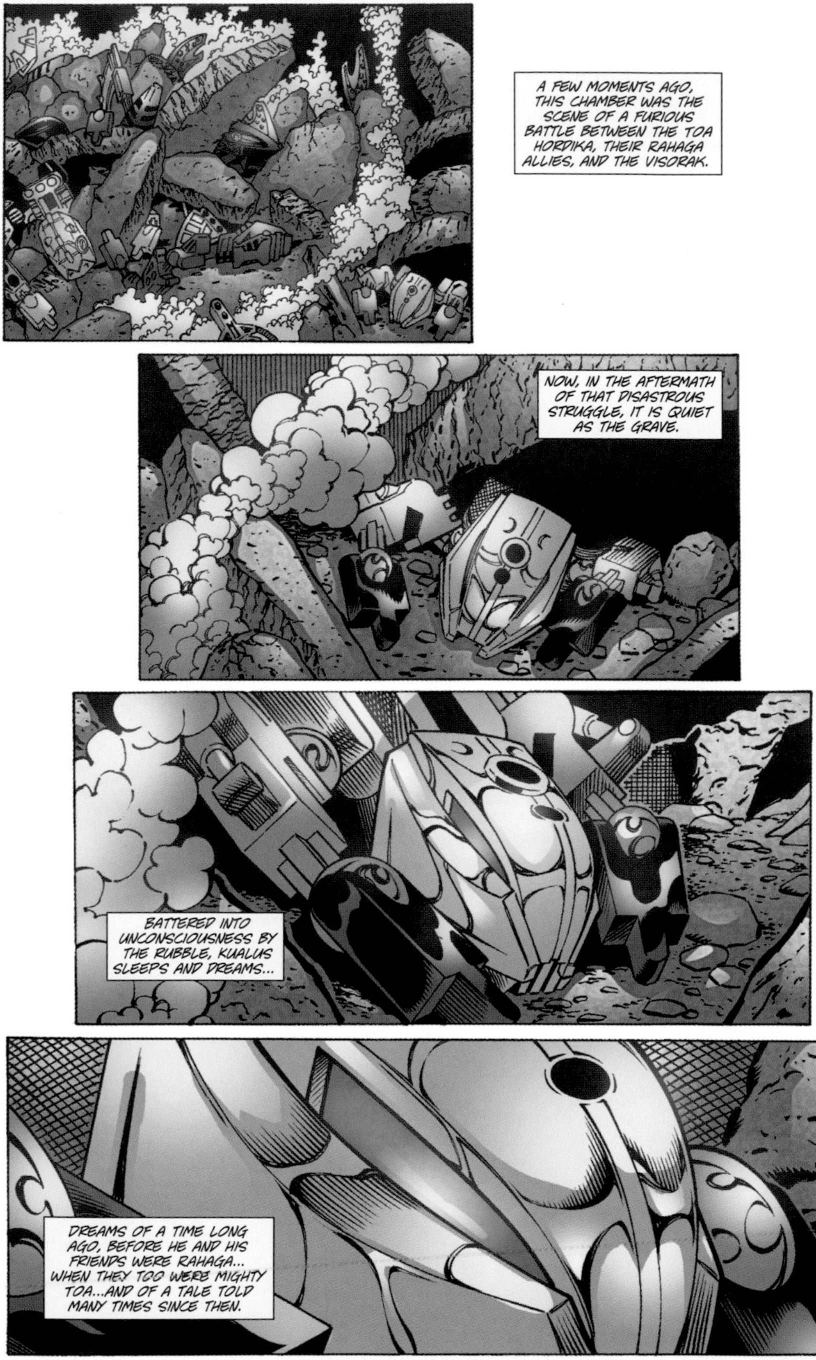
A FEW MOMENTS AGO, THIS CHAMBER WAS THE SCENE OF A FURIOUS BATTLE BETWEEN THE TOA HORDIKA, THEIR RAHAGA ALLIES, AND THE VISORAK.
NOW, IN THE AFTERMATH OF THAT DISASTROUS STRUGGLE, IT IS QUIET AS THE GRAVE.
BATTERED INTO UNCONSCIOUSNESS BY THE RUBBLE, KUALUS SLEEPS AND DREAMS...
DREAMS OF A TIME LONG AGO, BEFORE HE AND HIS FRIENDS WERE RAHAGA... WHEN THEY TOO WERE MIGHTY TOA...AND OF A TALE TOLD MANY TIMES SINCE THEN.

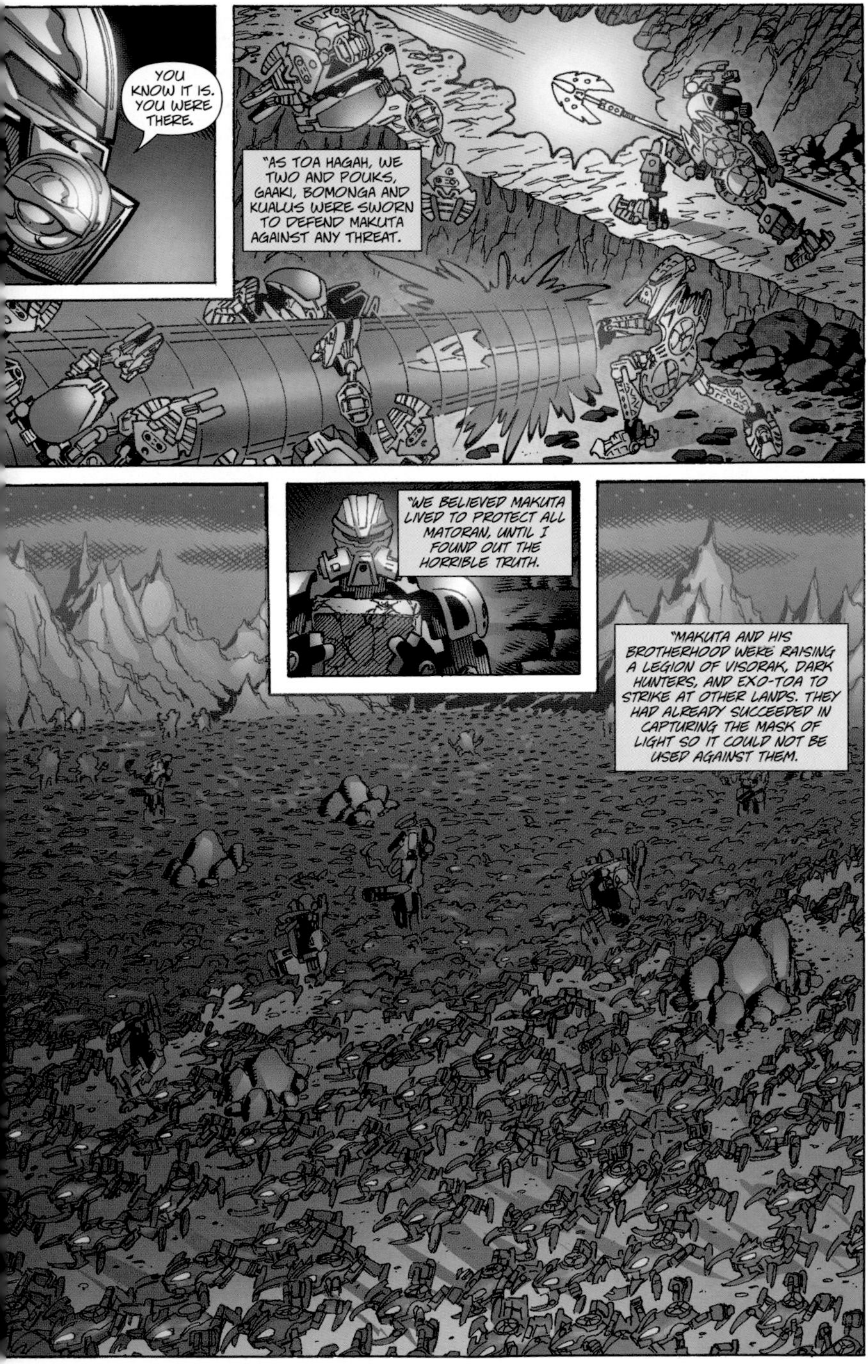
YOU KNOW IT IS. YOU WERE THERE.
"AS TOA HAGAH, WE TWO AND POUKS, GAAKI, BOMONGA AND KUALUS WERE SWORN TO DEFEND MAKUTA AGAINST ANY THREAT.
"WE BELIEVED MAKUTA LIVED TO PROTECT ALL MATORAN, UNTIL I FOUND OUT THE HORRIBLE TRUTH.
"MAKUTA AND HIS BROTHERHOOD WERE RAISING A LEGION OF VISORAK, DARK HUNTERS, AND EXO-TOA TO STRIKE AT OTHER LANDS. THEY HAD ALREADY SUCCEEDED IN CAPTURING THE MASK OF LIGHT SO IT COULD NOT BE USED AGAINST THEM.

"WE RAIDED THEIR FORTRESS, STOLE THE MASK BACK, AND MADE OUR ESCAPE."

FOUR CAPTURED TOA TO "QUESTION"--HOW DELICIOUS.

HOLD IT! LOOK OVER THERE!

LEAVING THE SUUKORAK BOUND AND HELPLESS, NORIK AND IRUINI TRAIL THE DARK HUNTER.

I DON'T SUPPOSE HE COULD BE TALKING ABOUT FOUR OTHER TOA?

IF YOU BELIEVED THAT, YOU WOULDN'T BE HERE. YOU TOLD ME YOU WERE GOING TO QUIT THE TEAM AFTER WE RAIDED THE BROTHERHOOD'S FORTRESS, REMEMBER?

AND I WILL--AS SOON AS THE OTHERS ARE SAFE.

CONCEALING THE MASK IN A SAFE PLACE, IRUINI USES HIS KANOHI MASK OF QUICK TRAVEL TO TELEPORT HIMSELF...

CAN I GET IN? I WAS SNEAKING INTO WORSE PLACES THAN THIS WHEN YOU WERE STILL TRYING TO MAKE SPARKS...

...AND REAPPEARS NEXT TO THE VISORAK CAGE.

NOT SURE WHO YOU ARE, BUT I'M HERE TO GET YOU OUT. AND HAVE YOU SEEN FOUR TOA?

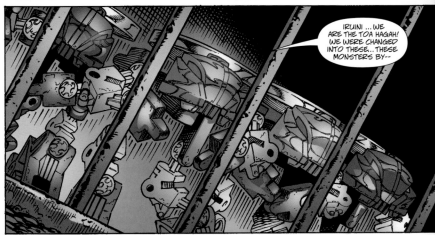

IRUINI ... WE ARE THE TOA HAGAH! WE WERE CHANGED INTO THESE... THESE MONSTERS BY--

UNNGHH!

KRA-KAM

BY ME!

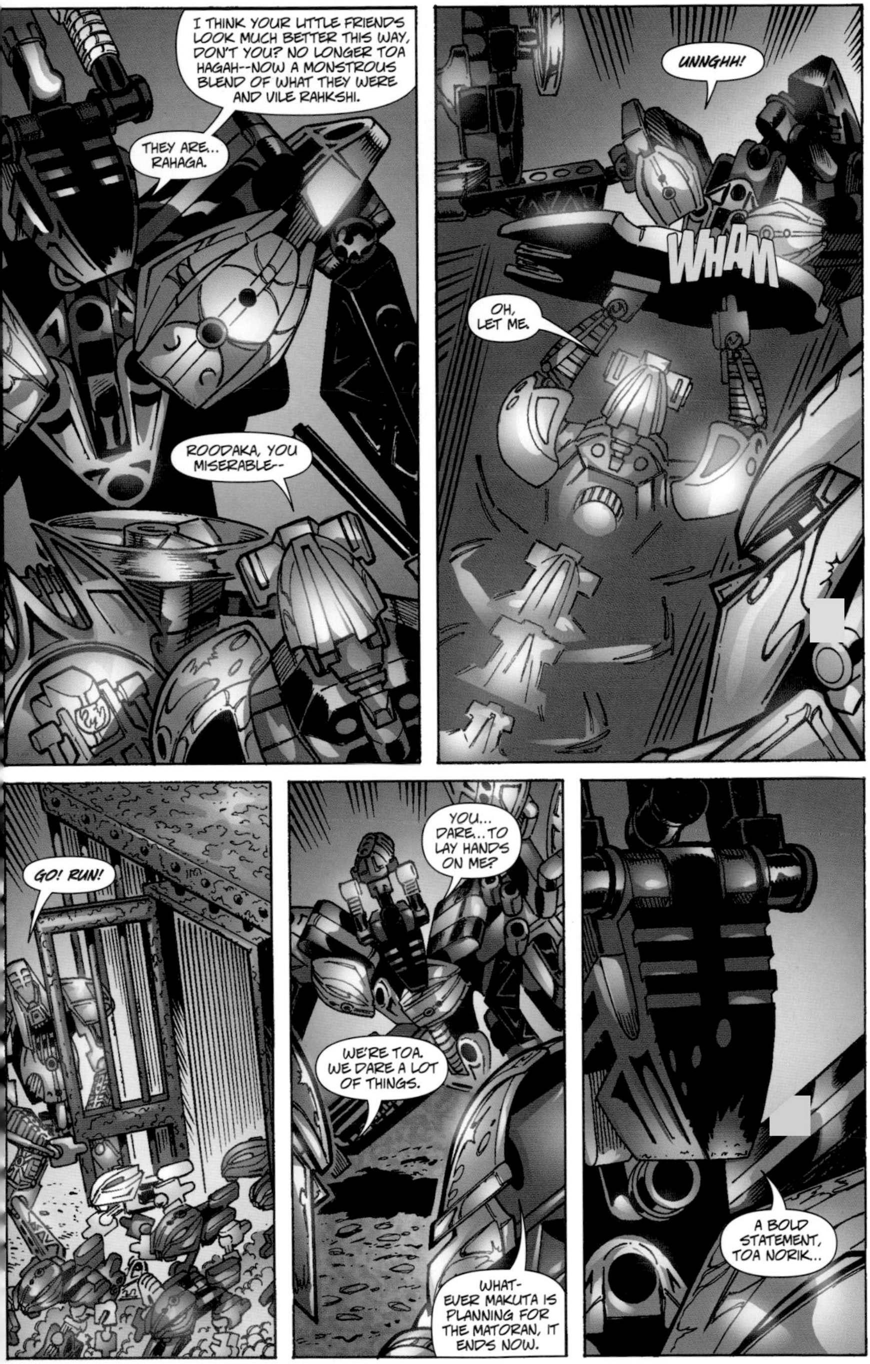
I THINK YOUR LITTLE FRIENDS LOOK MUCH BETTER THIS WAY, DON'T YOU? NO LONGER TOA HAGAH--NOW A MONSTROUS BLEND OF WHAT THEY WERE AND VILE RAHKSHI.
THEY ARE... RAHAGA.
ROODAKA, YOU MISERABLE--
UNNGHH!
WHAM
OH, LET ME.
GO! RUN!
YOU... DARE...TO LAY HANDS ON ME?
WE'RE TOA. WE DARE A LOT OF THINGS.
WHAT-EVER MAKUTA IS PLANNING FOR THE MATORAN, IT ENDS NOW.
A BOLD STATEMENT, TOA NORIK...

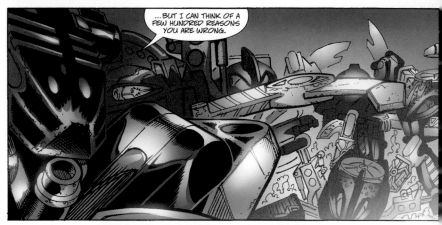

...BUT I CAN THINK OF A FEW HUNDRED REASONS YOU ARE WRONG.

THE OTHERS ARE SAFE. REMEMBER WHAT WE DID AGAINST THE FROSTELUS?

YOU CALL IT.

VWHOOSH

NOW!

USING THE CYCLONE OF MOLTEN LAVA TO DISTRACT THE VISORAK, THE TWO TOA HAGAH RACE TO JOIN THEIR TEAMMATES.

BUT NO AMOUNT OF MAGMA CAN STOP ROODAKA'S RHOTUKA SPINNERS.

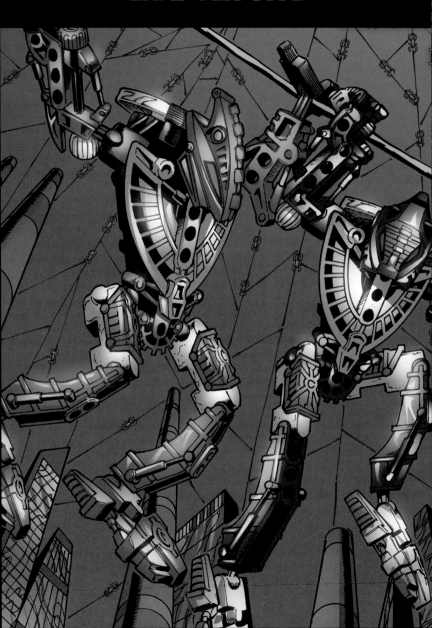

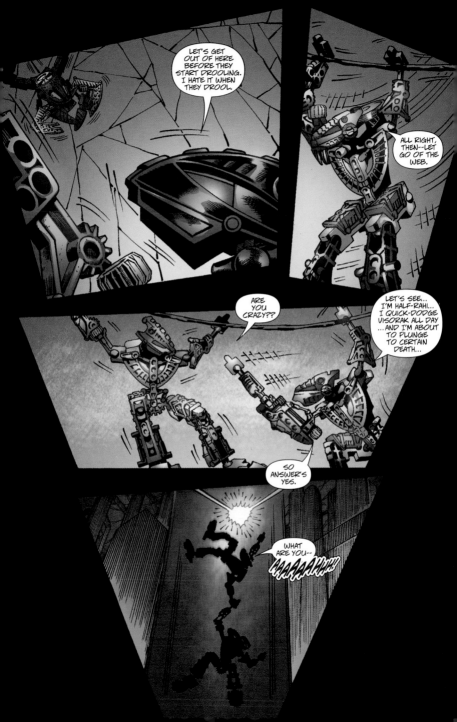

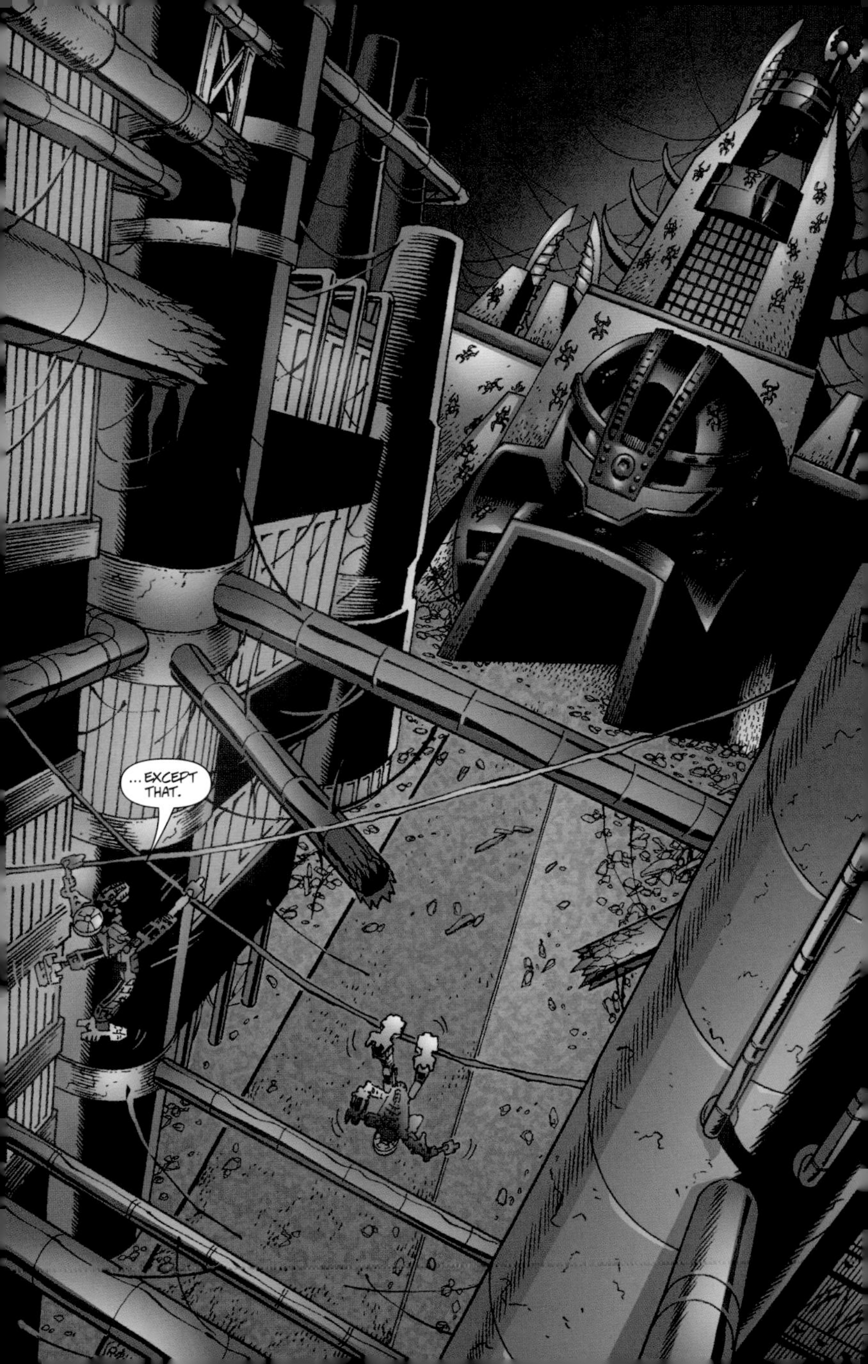
...EXCEPT THAT.

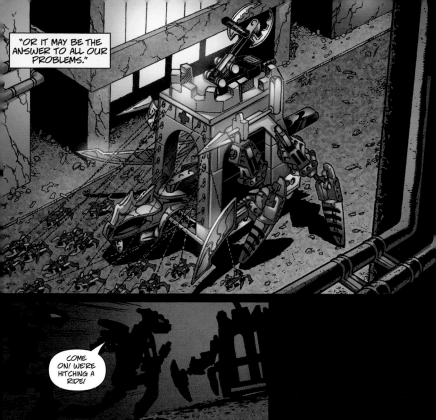

"OR IT MAY BE THE ANSWER TO ALL OUR PROBLEMS."

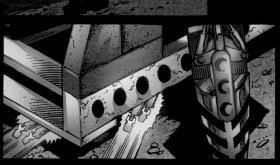

COME ON! WE'RE HITCHING A RIDE!

WHAT IF THEY TRY TO RAM SOMETHING WHILE WE'RE UNDER HERE?

THEN WE WILL HAVE A MUCH FASTER-- AND SHORTER-- TRIP.

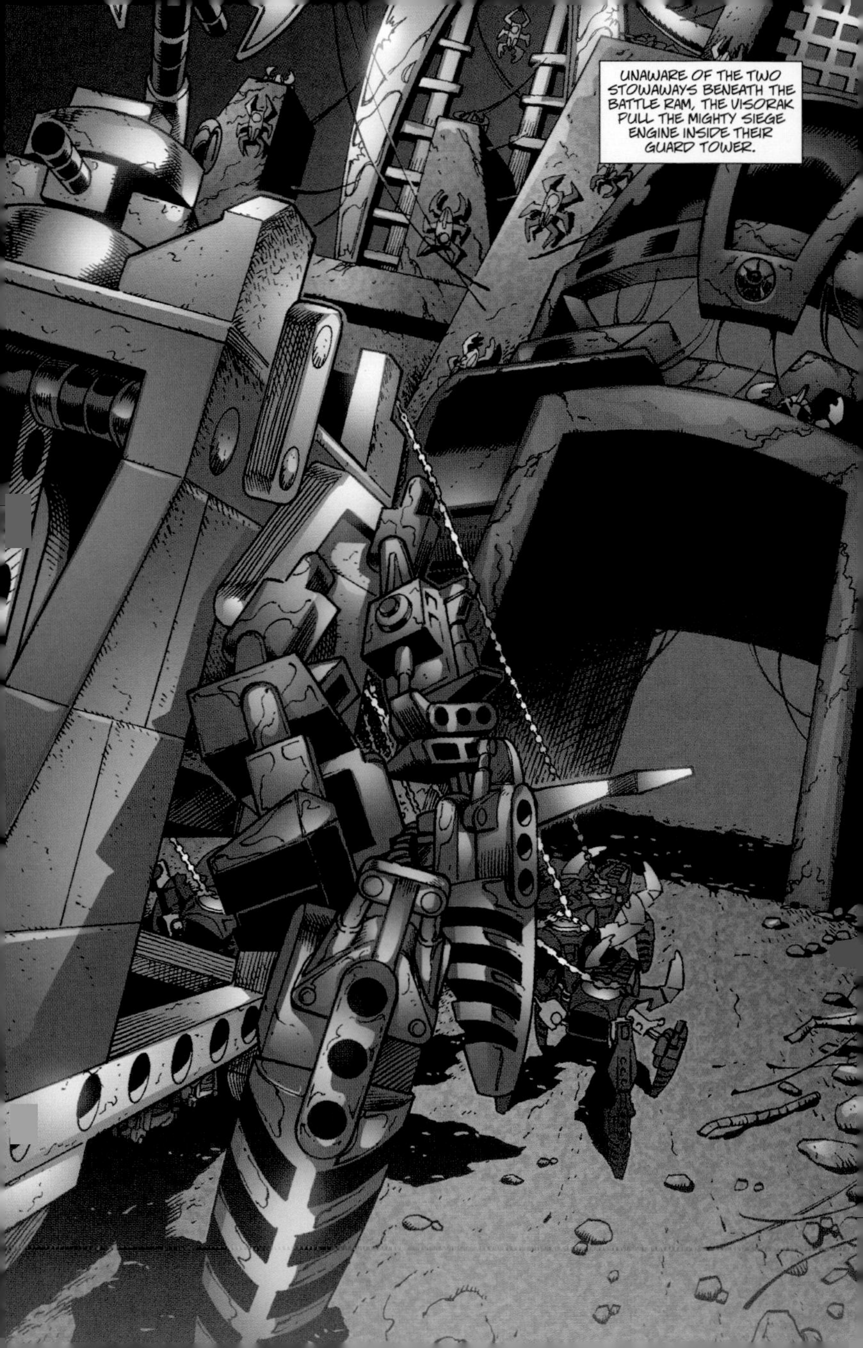
UNAWARE OF THE TWO STOWAWAYS BENEATH THE BATTLE RAM, THE VISORAK PULL THE MIGHTY SIEGE ENGINE INSIDE THEIR GUARD TOWER.

END CHAPTER FIVE

TRIAL BY FIRE
CHAPTER SIX

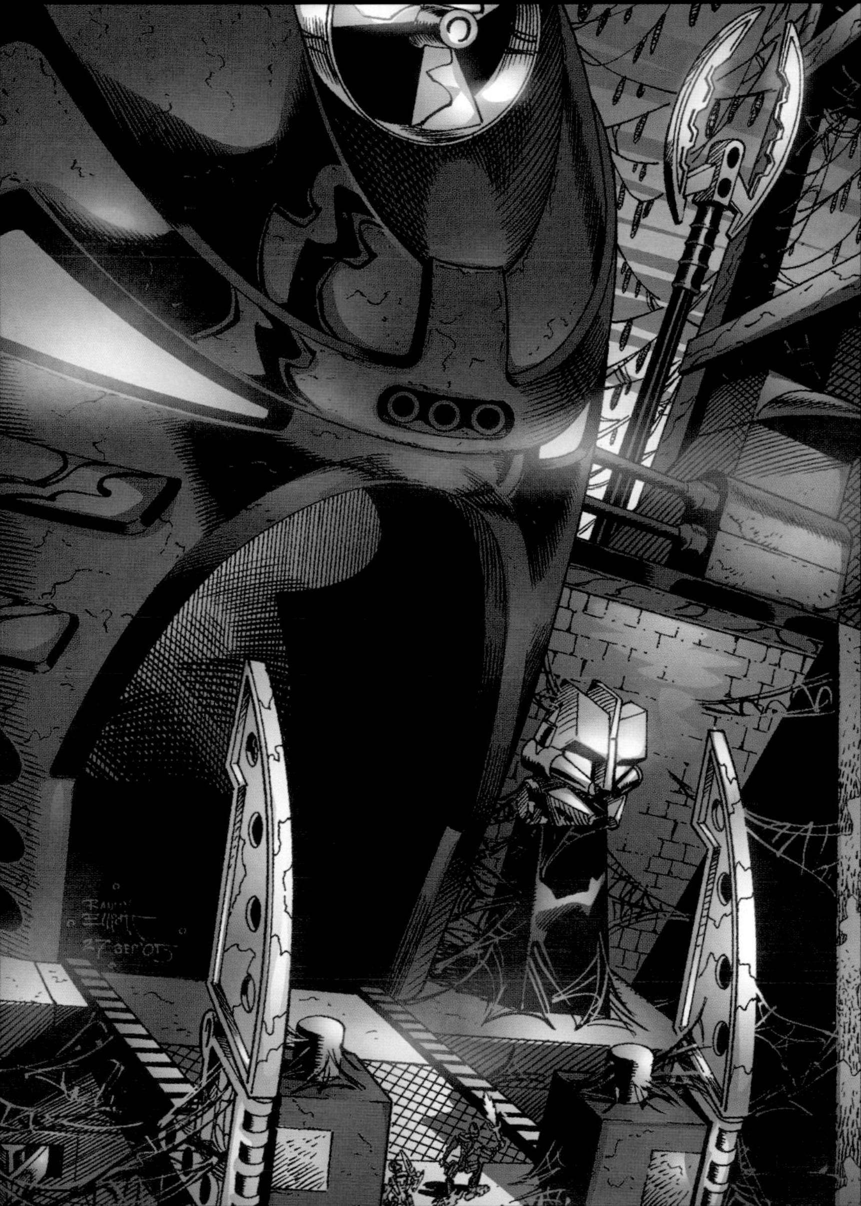

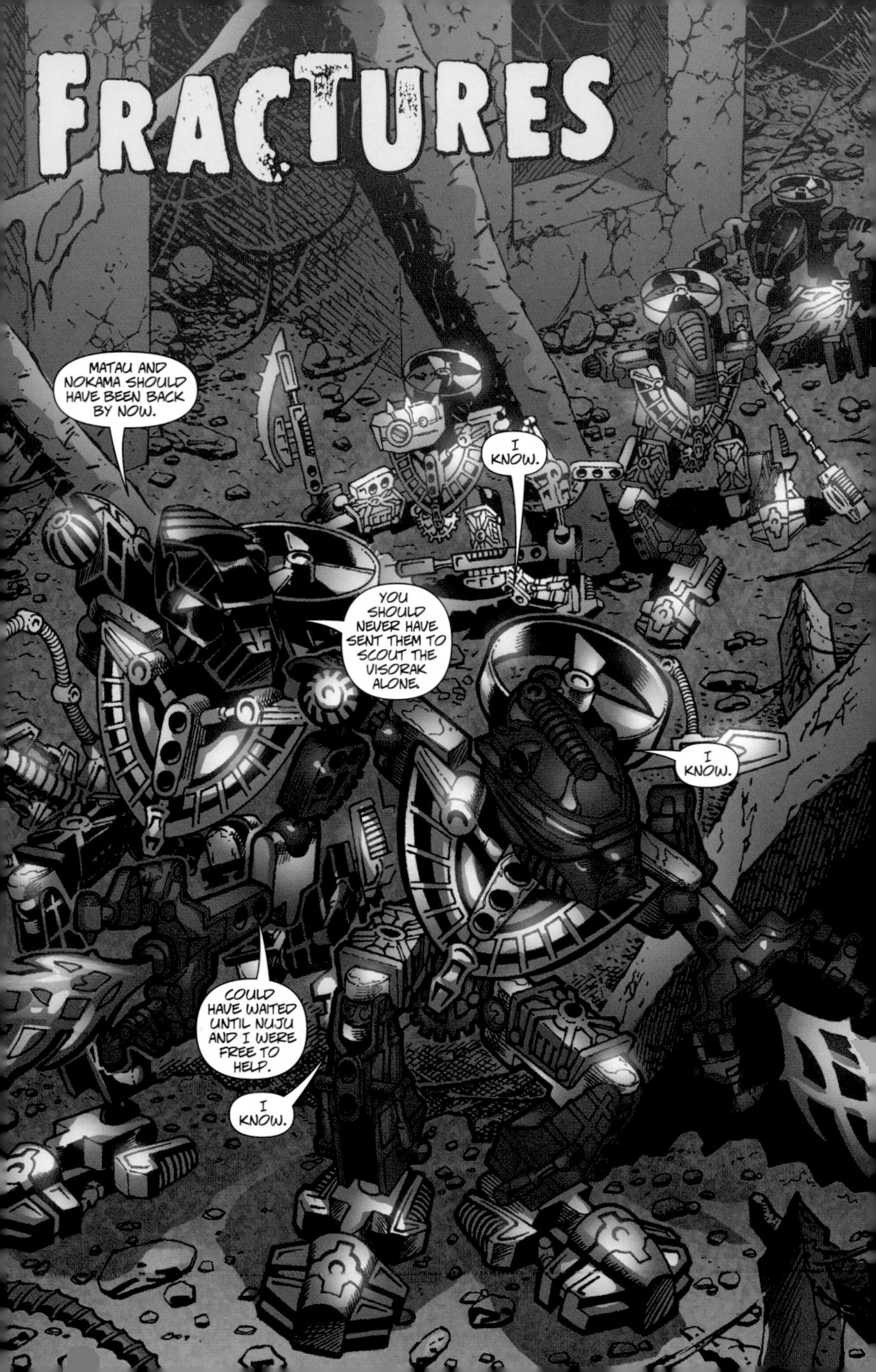
FRACTURES
MATAU AND NOKAMA SHOULD HAVE BEEN BACK BY NOW.
I KNOW.
YOU SHOULD NEVER HAVE SENT THEM TO SCOUT THE VISORAK ALONE.
I KNOW.
COULD HAVE WAITED UNTIL NUJU AND I WERE FREE TO HELP.
I KNOW.

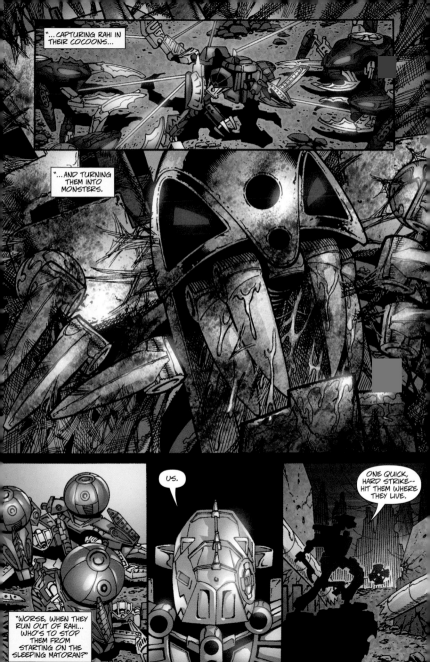

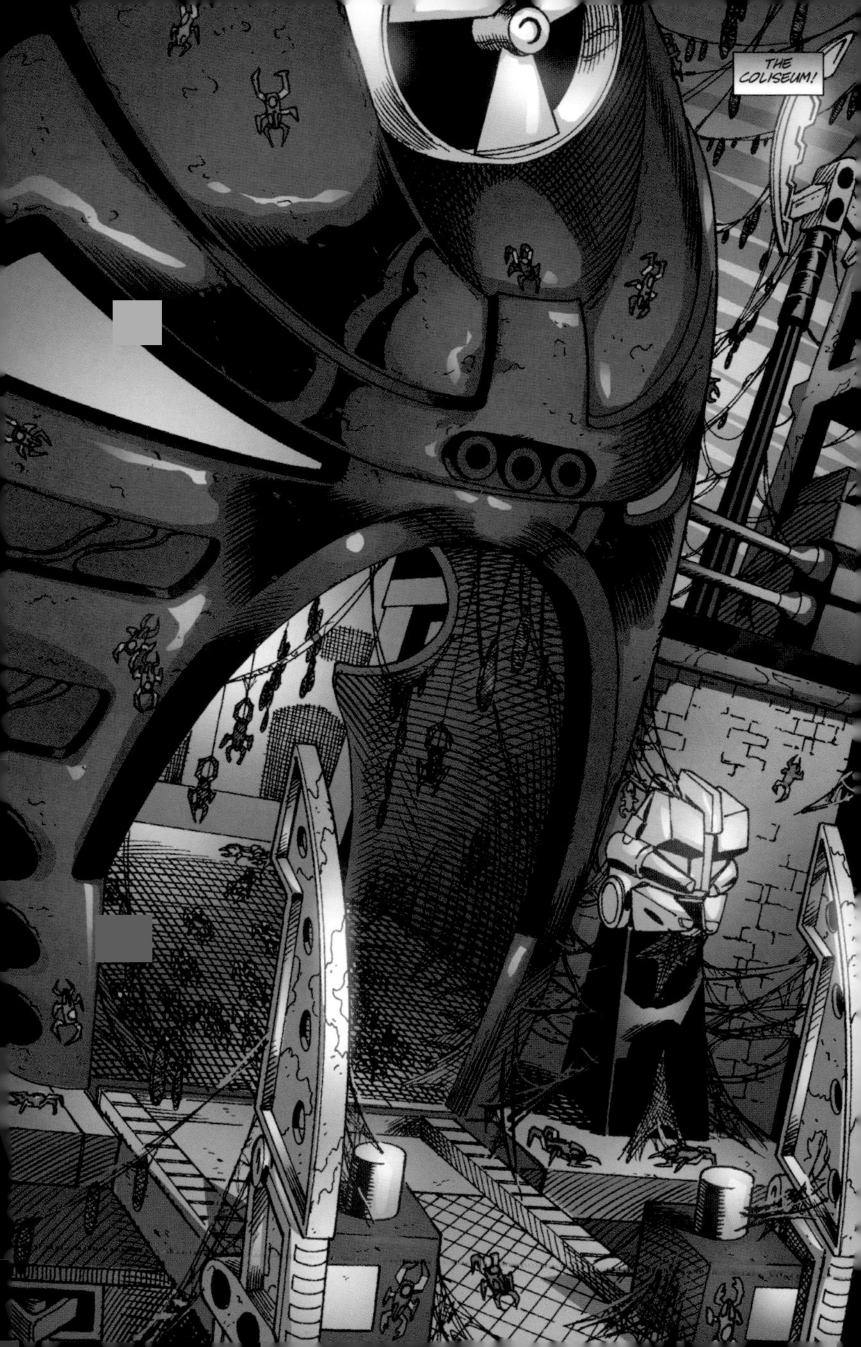
THE COLISEUM!

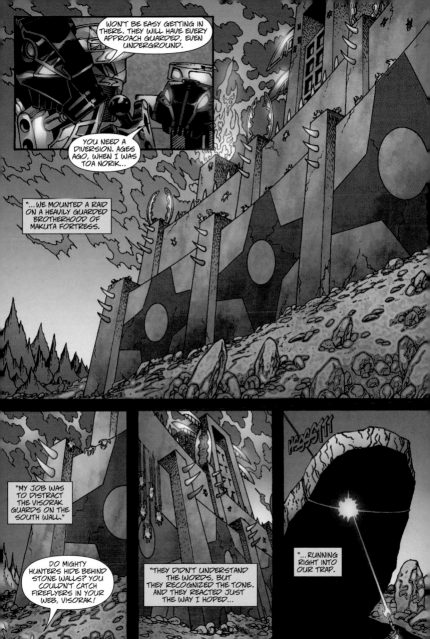

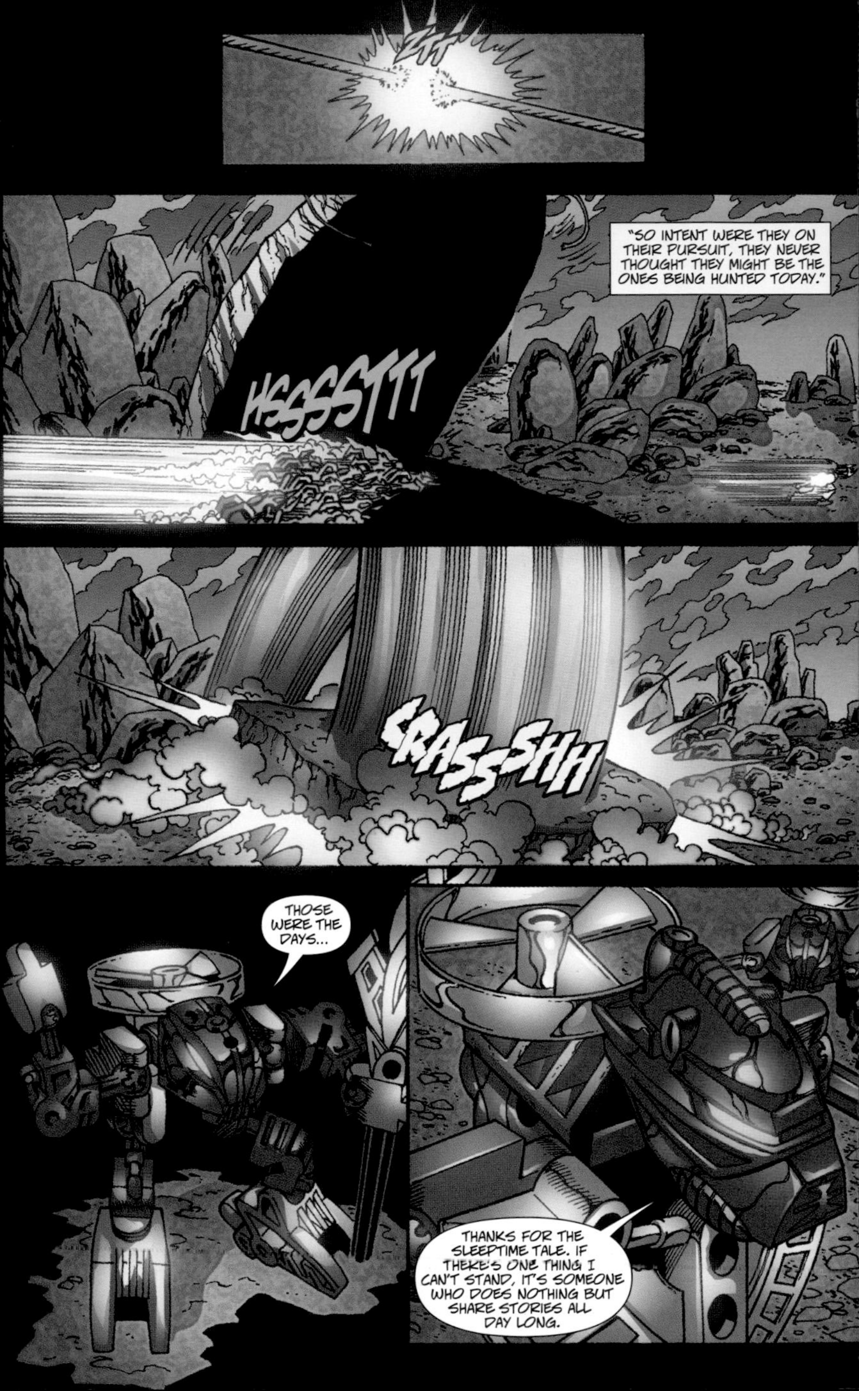
ZAT
"SO INTENT WERE THEY ON THEIR PURSUIT, THEY NEVER THOUGHT THEY MIGHT BE THE ONES BEING HUNTED TODAY."
HSSSSTTT
CRASSSHH
THOSE WERE THE DAYS...
THANKS FOR THE SLEEPTIME TALE. IF THERE'S ONE THING I CAN'T STAND, IT'S SOMEONE WHO DOES NOTHING BUT SHARE STORIES ALL DAY LONG.

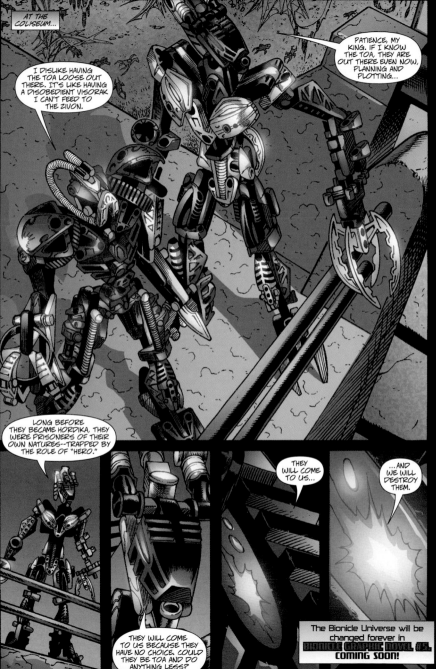

WATCH OUT FOR PAPERCUTZ™

Welcome to a scary edition of the Papercutz Backpages, the place to find out all the latest news about the graphic novel publishers of THE HARDY BOYS, NANCY DREW, TALES FROM THE CRYPT, BIONICLE, and CLASSICS ILLUSTRATED. I'm Jim Salicrup, your Editor-in-Chief, and prime Papercutz promoter! We've got lots to talk about, so let's get right to it...

Things have taken a scary turn here at Papercutz! Don't panic --we're not talking about any of our graphic novels suddenly vanishing from bookstore shelves! We're not talking that kind of scary! Thanks to your continued support, our sales are stronger than ever, and if any of our titles have vanished off the shelves, it's only because they are temporarily sold out! No, we're talking TALES FROM THE CRYPT scary -- and how it's suddenly seeming to take over the pages of CLASSICS ILLUSTRATED and CLASSICS ILLUSTRATED DELUXE!

CLASSICS ILLUSTRATED #4 features world-famous cartoonist Gahan Wilson's creepy cartoons illustrated Edgar Allan Poe's "The Raven and Other Poems." And if that wasn't scary enough, CLASSICS ILLUSTRAT-ED DELUXE #3 features an all-new adaptation by Marion Mousse of Mary Shelly's monster-masterwork "Frankenstein"!

Why have our CLASSICS ILLUSTRATED titles turned into a virtual vault of horror? The answer is obvious! After all, what is a "classic" if not a story so powerfully compelling that it leads to countless retellings? But we suspect that you've never experienced Poe's poems as seen through macabre cartoonist Gahan Wilson's bloodshot eyes, or the tale of Victor Frankenstein and his monster as dramatically brought to life, so to speak, by the dark visions of Marion Mousse.

Despite how many times the Frankenstein story has been told, it's as thought-provoking and as frightening now as the day it was when originally published in 1818. If you've never read the original novel you may be surprised that it's not the over-the-top crazy story so many adaptations may imply, but rather it's a serious tale tackling many major issues. Mousse takes great pains to restore many of Victor Frankenstein's motivations that lead to his "mad quest" to solve the ultimate mystery of life and death (as opposed to simply creating a monster).

In the pages that follow you'll see for yourself, the skill and artistry that Mousse brings to faithfully adapting this terrifying classic. Keep in mind, that the pages of CLASSICS ILLUSTRATED DELUXE are much larger than these pages, so to truly savor these pages, and to avoid eyestrain, be sure to pick up CLASSICS ILLUSTRATED DELUXE #3!

Thanks,

JIM

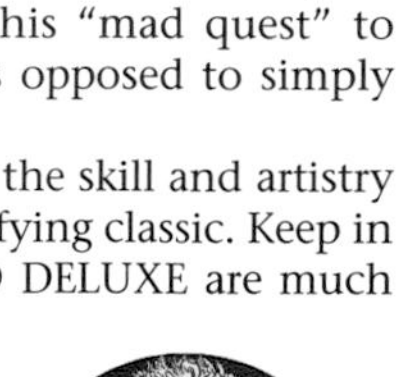

THE OLD EDITOR

Caricature by Rick Parker

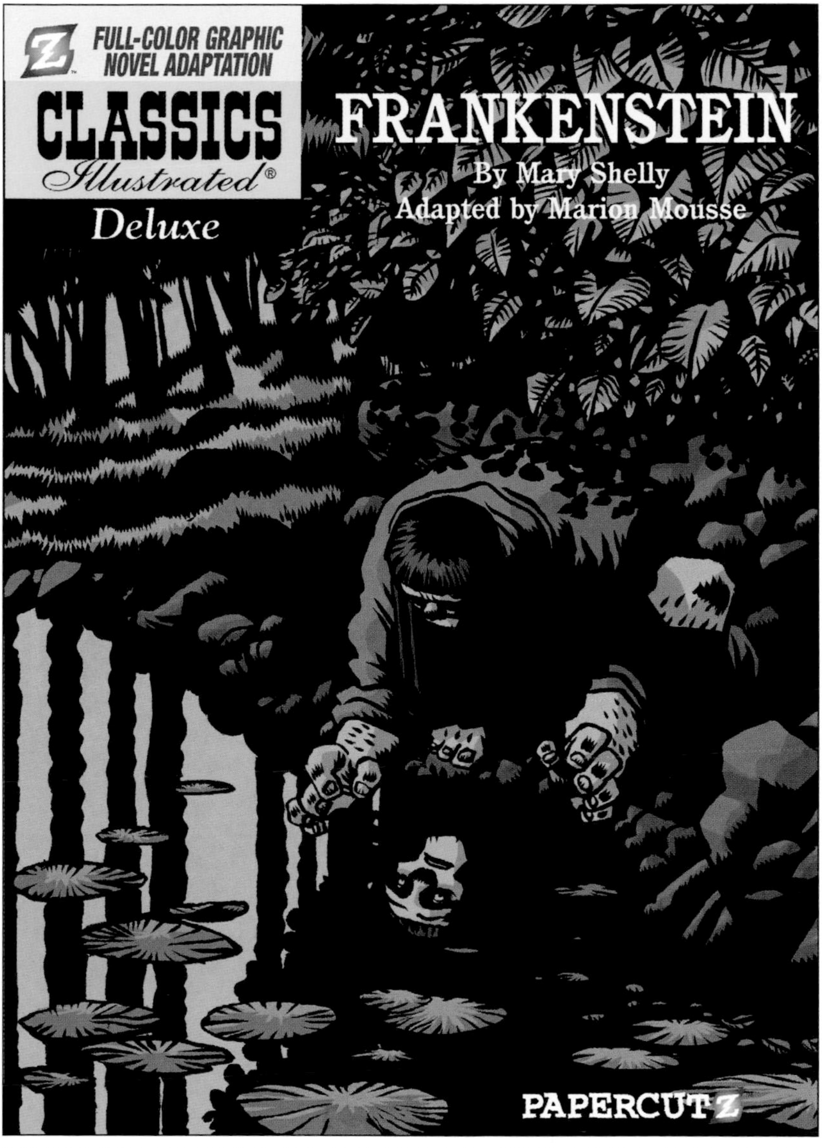
FULL-COLOR GRAPHIC NOVEL ADAPTATION
CLASSICS Illustrated®
Deluxe
FRANKENSTEIN
By Mary Shelly
Adapted by Marion Mousse
PAPERCUTZ

FOR MORE THAN A YEAR, I STUDIED ALL THE FORMS AND CONSEQUENCES OF DEATH: THE FLESH DECOMPOSING, SLOWLY ROTTING...

...THE MATTER OF WHICH WE'RE ALL MADE, DEGRADING AND WASTING AWAY BEFORE VANISHING AS THOUGH THROUGH MAGIC.

FRANKENSTEIN...

...OUR LOCAL CELEBRITY HARD AT WORK.

...

DOCTOR KREMPE...

YOUR WHIMSICAL THEORIES ARE THE MOCKERY OF ALL INGOLSTADT, FRANKENSTEIN!

WHY THEN? IF YOU PREFER DIGGING THROUGH FLESH TO DELIGHTING IN THAT CREDULOUS AUDIENCE.

STILL CHASING AFTER YOUR MAD HEROES?! CORNELIUS AGRIPPA, PARACELSUS...

DON'T TELL ME THAT YOU'RE STILL A DISCIPLE OF THOSE COOKED-UP ABSURDITIES?!

PHILLIPUS AUREOLUS VON HOHENHEIM, KNOWN AS PARACELSUS, EMINENT ALCHEMIST, WHO CLAIMED TO HAVE EXPERIMENTED ON THE FAMOUS ELIXIR OF ETERNAL YOUTH AND CREATED...

...THE HOMUNCULUS, A SMALL LIVING BEING IN THE FORM OF A HUMAN!

I KNOW ALL THAT, FRANKENSTEIN!

SO YOU CONTINUE AND CONTINUE TO PERSIST! YOU PERSIST IN RIDICULING YOUR PROFESSORS, IN DISCREDITING OUR HONORABLE INSTITUTION?!!

WELL THEN! SO, I HEREAFTER FORBID YOU TO USE COURSE MATERIAL SUCH AS HUMAN REMAINS OUTSIDE OF YOUR COURSES!

UNTIL NOW, I'D MADE NO ASSUMPTIONS ABOUT YOUR CHARACTER, YOUNG MAN.

YES, I WAS HESITATING...I WAS HESITATING BETWEEN A YAHOO AND AN ENLIGHTENED SCIENTIST...NOW I KNOW.

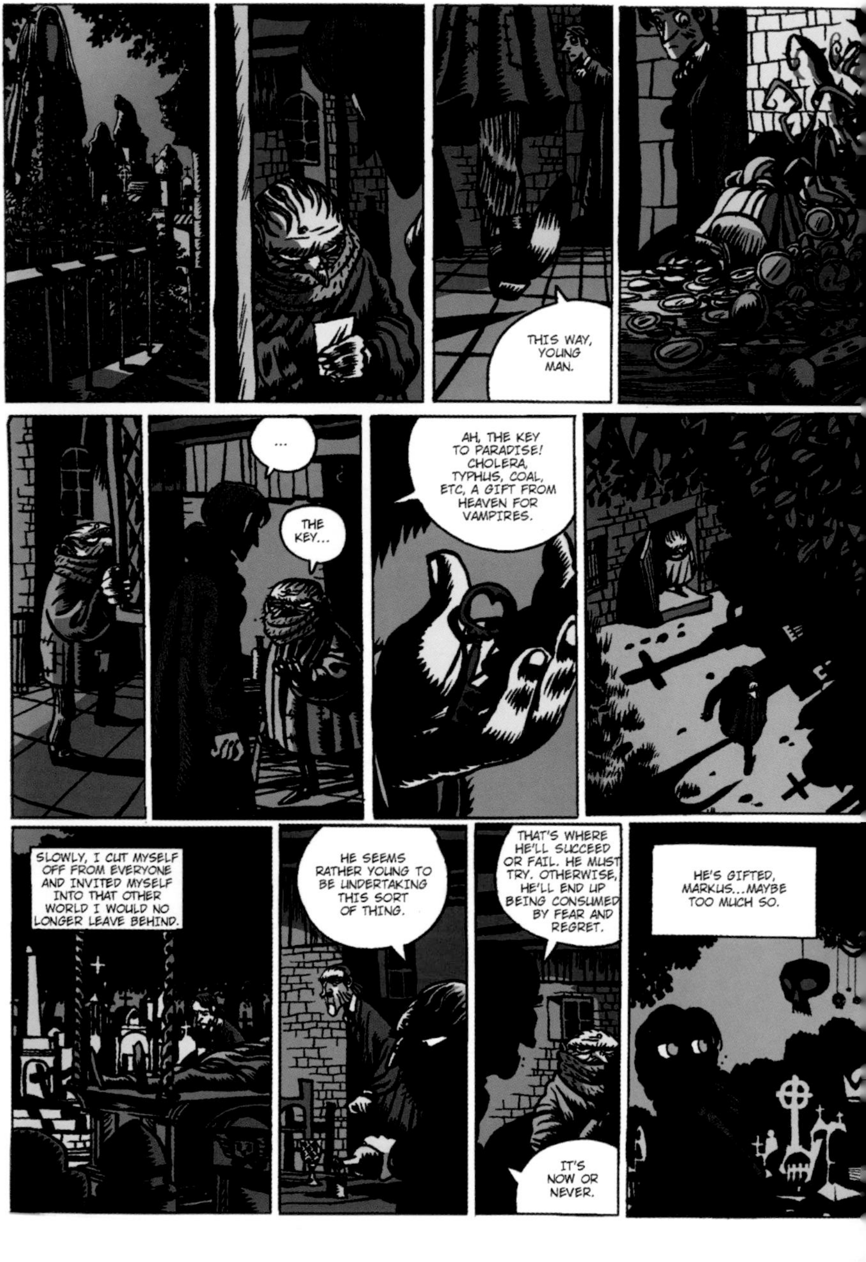
THIS WAY, YOUNG MAN.
...
THE KEY...
AH, THE KEY TO PARADISE! CHOLERA, TYPHUS, COAL, ETC, A GIFT FROM HEAVEN FOR VAMPIRES.
SLOWLY, I CUT MYSELF OFF FROM EVERYONE AND INVITED MYSELF INTO THAT OTHER WORLD I WOULD NO LONGER LEAVE BEHIND.
HE SEEMS RATHER YOUNG TO BE UNDERTAKING THIS SORT OF THING.
THAT'S WHERE HE'LL SUCCEED OR FAIL. HE MUST TRY. OTHERWISE, HE'LL END UP BEING CONSUMED BY FEAR AND REGRET.
IT'S NOW OR NEVER.
HE'S GIFTED, MARKUS...MAYBE TOO MUCH SO.

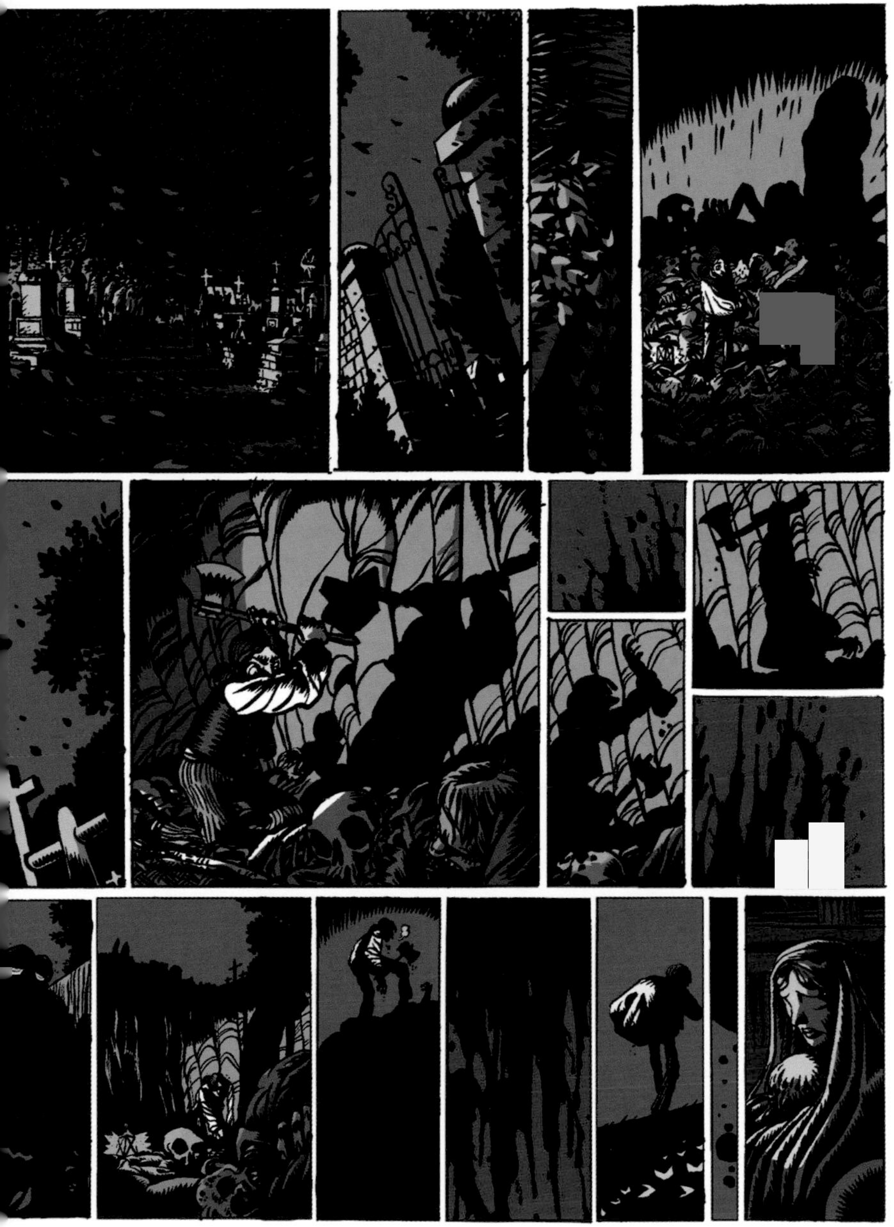

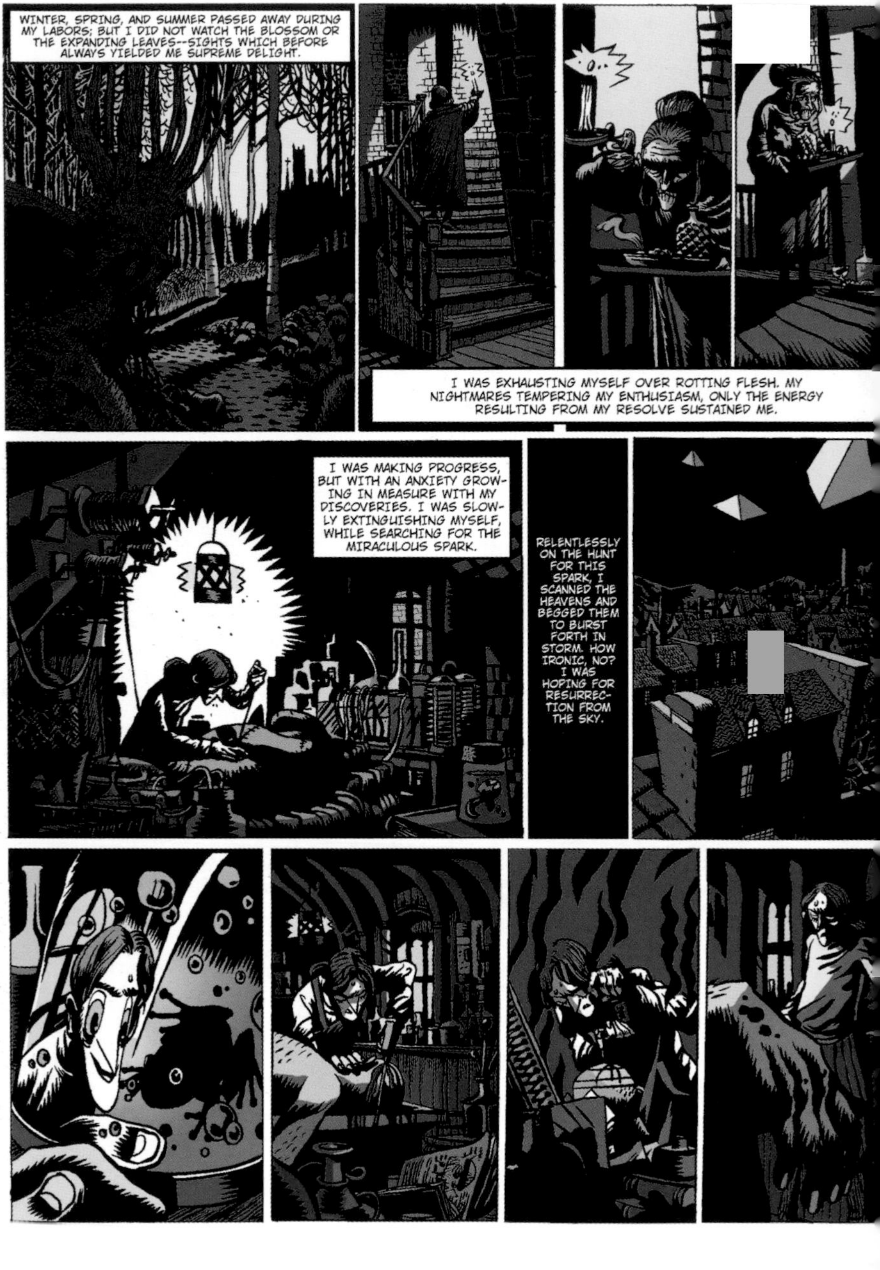

WINTER, SPRING, AND SUMMER PASSED AWAY DURING MY LABORS; BUT I DID NOT WATCH THE BLOSSOM OR THE EXPANDING LEAVES--SIGHTS WHICH BEFORE ALWAYS YIELDED ME SUPREME DELIGHT.
I WAS EXHAUSTING MYSELF OVER ROTTING FLESH. MY NIGHTMARES TEMPERING MY ENTHUSIASM, ONLY THE ENERGY RESULTING FROM MY RESOLVE SUSTAINED ME.
I WAS MAKING PROGRESS, BUT WITH AN ANXIETY GROWING IN MEASURE WITH MY DISCOVERIES. I WAS SLOWLY EXTINGUISHING MYSELF, WHILE SEARCHING FOR THE MIRACULOUS SPARK.
RELENTLESSLY ON THE HUNT FOR THIS SPARK, I SCANNED THE HEAVENS AND BEGGED THEM TO BURST FORTH IN STORM. HOW IRONIC, NO? I WAS HOPING FOR RESURRECTION FROM THE SKY.

Don't miss CLASSICS ILLUSTRATED DELUXE #3 – "Frankenstein"

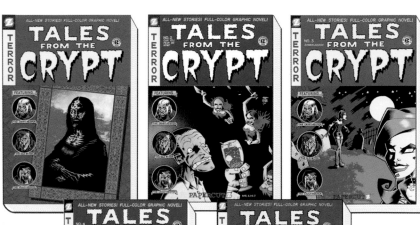

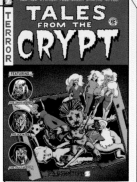

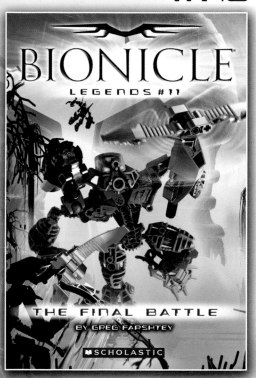

BIONICLE®

LEGENDS

WHO WILL LIVE?
WHO WILL DIE?

BIONICLE
LEGENDS #11
THE FINAL BATTLE
BY GREG FARSHTEY
SCHOLASTIC

The Toa Nuva challenge the Brotherhood of Makuta for the fate of the Great Spirit. When the final battle is over, everything in the BIONICLE universe will be changed forever!

THE SPECTACULAR SERIES-ENDING FINALE!

AVAILABLE WHEREVER BOOKS ARE SOLD

SCHOLASTIC

www.scholastic.com
www.lego.com

LEGO

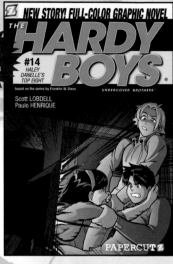

NOT SO VERY LONG AGO, SIX CANISTERS WASHED UP ON THE SHORES OF AN ISLAND CALLED MATA NUI...

SIX HEROES EMERGED FROM THOSE CANISTERS AND DARED TO CHALLENGE THE DARKNESS.

BUT THESE CANISTERS DO NOT CARRY TOA... AND THIS IS NOT MATA NUI...

SKRIEK

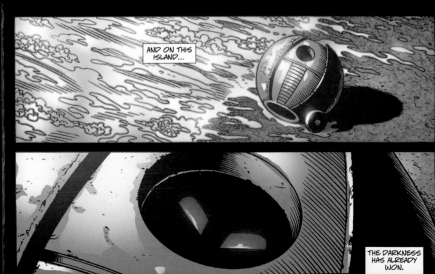

AND ON THIS ISLAND...

THE DARKNESS HAS ALREADY WON.